MADE IN SATURN

MADE IN SATURN

Rita Indiana

Translated from the Spanish
by Sydney Hutchinson

SHEFFIELD – LONDON – NEW YORK

First published in English in 2020 by And Other Stories
Sheffield – London – New York
www.andotherstories.org

First published as *Hecho en Saturno* by Editorial Periférica in 2018
Copyright © Rita Indiana c/o Schavelzon Graham Agencia Literaria, 2020
English-language translation © Sydney Hutchinson, 2020

9 8 7 6 5 4 3 2 1

ISBN: 9781911508601
eBook ISBN: 9781911508618

Editor: Bella Bosworth; Copy-editor: Gesche Ipsen; Proofreader: Sarah Terry; Typesetter:
Tetragon, London; Typefaces: Linotype Neue Swift and Verlag; Cover design: Steven
Marsden. Printed and bound by CPI Group (UK) Ltd, Croydon, CRO 4YY.

A catalogue record for this book is available from the British Library.

And Other Stories gratefully acknowledge that our work is supported using public
funding by Arts Council England.

In memory of Milagros Dottin

Come down off your throne and leave your body alone
Somebody must change
You are the reason I've been waiting so long
Somebody holds the key
Well, I'm near the end and I just ain't got the time
And I'm wasted and I can't find my way home.

'CAN'T FIND MY WAY HOME', BLIND FAITH

Doctor's office light. Dull light, wet behind a hood of clouds that sank the shoulders of the horizon. Dull, like the orthopaedic shoes of Dr. Bengoa, like the folder on which the doctor had written the name of his new patient, Argenis Luna, who was just coming off a Cubana Airlines flight, dizzy and dripping a pasty, cold sweat. Bengoa was waiting for him on the tarmac in his wrinkled, champagne-colored *guayabera* shirt, both hands on a sign whose bold letters he had filled in impeccably.

As soon as he recognized Argenis, the doctor came over to take his pulse while looking at his wristwatch. As they walked down the tarmac to pick up his bags he introduced him to the young soldier escorting them, saying, "This is the son of José Alfredo Luna." The palm trees defied the lightning's flashes against the gray background of the clouds, and in spite of his malaise Argenis thought it was beautiful. The air was charged and he breathed with difficulty, his nose running like an open faucet. Now at the baggage carousel, Bengoa spoke again to the soldier, adding, "My comrade José Alfredo is a hero of the Dominican urban guerrilla war and a student of Professor Juan Bosch."

Argenis's bags dropped out onto the carousel just as Bosch surfaced into the conversation. They rode all the way around before he could be bothered to identify them, before he could be bothered to interrupt Bengoa. The heroic attributes Dr. Bengoa was listing orbited eternally around his father's legend, and Argenis along with them, just another satellite, like the red fabric suitcases on the belt. He had no strength to grab them, full as they were of the stuff his mother had bought to outfit his detox treatment in Cuba. He pointed them out with his finger and pulled the hood of his jacket up to combat the air-conditioning and the embarrassment of his obvious weakness. For months he had been living on the sofas of those friends who could still stand him, his only property a green Eastpak backpack he used to hold his syringes, his spoon, and a Case Logic full of CDs. His mother had thrown everything into the trash except the CDs and the backpack, which now held a bottle of Barceló Imperial rum as a gift for Dr. Bengoa and a big box of Frosted Flakes.

The young soldier helped them carry the bags to the car, the muscles of his lower arms barely contracting from the weight of the luggage. He feigned enthusiasm for Bengoa's topic and looked at Argenis out of the corner of his eye, as if trying to find something of the heroic father in the 120 pounds of skin and bones his son amounted to that spring.

From far away Dr. Bengoa's brick-red Lada looked new, but now inside, suffering a chill of the sort that precedes diarrhea, Argenis calculated the real age of the car by the cracks in the dashboard. He had gone forty-eight hours without heroin and had thrown up in the airplane. The Cuban flight attendants with their anachronistic uniforms and hairstyles had seemed as absurd to him as the Alka-Seltzer tablets they offered to relieve his symptoms.

Dr. Bengoa opened the glove compartment with a whack of his hand and extracted a disposable needle, some cotton, a length of rubber, and a strip of amber-colored capsules that said "Temgesic 3mg." The strip fell onto Argenis's lap and for the first time he noticed the dirt that had accumulated on his jeans. They were the same ones he had been wearing a little less than a month ago when he moved into his pusher Rambo's house.

As he tied the rubber strap around Argenis's left arm to make the vein pop out, Dr. Bengoa explained the details of his stay, and then, pushing the syringe into the ampoule, he said, "It's buprenorphine, a synthetic morphine used to treat addiction." Bengoa injected him right there in the José Martí airport parking lot, with all the tranquility and legality his profession permitted, and Argenis let him do his job like a girl in love while taxi drivers in Cadillacs from a bygone era came and went, full of nostalgia tourists. Argenis had assumed that his treatment would be one of pain and abstinence, but there he was on his way to La Pradera, a hotel-turned-clinic for the health tourists who came to Cuba from all over the world, completely relieved of his symptoms and feeling how the chemical made ideas and objects lose their borders, their sharp edges.

From the outside at least, the complex looked like a cheap all-inclusive resort, one of the ones that fill up with middle-class families during Holy Week in Puerto Plata. The walls along the hallway to the reception area were decorated with posters of communist solidarity. Argenis tried unsuccessfully to imagine a hotel like this in the Dominican Republic. Colorful prints with maps and flags representing the various peoples of the world paid homage to the medical profession as a revolutionary bastion. On one of them, orange liquid from an immense syringe was being injected into a map of Latin America, with Haiti as the fortunate vein. At any other time Argenis would have made a joke.

11

Right in front of the injection poster, an older woman with an Argentine accent was asking a nurse for information about Coppelia, the ice-cream parlor, and next to her a younger woman who resembled her sat in a wheelchair, hiding the baldness of chemotherapy under a Mickey Mouse cap. Haydee, as the ID badge clipped to the nurse's shirt read, was not in uniform but was wearing those rubber-soled shoes that only gardeners or health professionals wore back then – everything-proof moccasins that had come from outside the country, the product of a night spent with a European, a satisfied patient's appreciation, or the guilty conscience of a sister exiled in Miami.

The nurse watched Bengoa with smiling complicity as she told the women about the history of the famous ice-cream parlor. She pulled a heavy wooden key ring with the number nineteen painted on it from her pocket and handed it to the doctor, saying "the lock has a trick to it," before helping the Argentines into a taxi.

The new chemical was entering his system to the hurried rhythm of Bengoa's conversation: a torrent of dates emblematic of the anti-imperialist struggle; recipes for detox shakes; bits of songs by Silvio, Amaury Pérez, and Los Guaraguao; the Chinese economy; and baseball statistics. His mouth was dry and his pupils so dilated that everything around him was starting to look like a high-contrast photo. He held on to the doctor's arm as they walked around the pool to room nineteen. The room, which Bengoa had called a privilege, had a view of the pool and a sliding glass door, in front of which two men, one in pajamas and the other in a bathing suit, were playing cards at a little wrought-iron table topped with plastic flowers. The doctor struggled with the lock, unable to hit on the trick Haydee had mentioned, while Argenis took stock of the

12

furnishings of his new room through the glass: a ceiling fan, twin beds, a nightstand.

The door to his pusher Rambo's house also had a trick to it: you had to pull on it as you inserted the key. "Let me try," he said to Bengoa, and the doctor moved aside, satisfied with the noticeable improvement in his new patient. Argenis tried once, twice, wiggling the key in the lock like the tail of a happy dog until the door gave way and the smell of bleach and clean sheets hit them in the face.

Privilege. He could feel the word in his mouth, as it made the same movements it would make to taste and swallow a spoonful of frosting. He said it every morning after brushing his teeth and washing his face, as he put on the tiny Speedos his mother had picked out. Then he would swim a bit, not very athletically, doing a few laps of breaststroke. Bengoa had prescribed it to stimulate his appetite and it was working. Around eight a.m., Haydee would bring a tray of fried eggs, toast, and coffee that he'd scarf down in his room without being able to avoid thinking about the people outside the clinic, people who mainly breakfasted on a watery coffee of chickpeas and old grounds.

"Eat it all up, Argenis," Haydee would tenderly request as she filled her bag with paper from the bathroom trash-can to throw out. Argenis wondered if Haydee lived in La Pradera or if she took the patients' leftovers home every night. Her rubber-soled shoes were as hygienic as they were discreet and they didn't reveal much beyond the work that allowed her to have them. They would never let on what Haydee thought of the foreigners whose dollars gave them access to places and services Cubans couldn't even dream of. According to Bengoa, Argenis wasn't in La Pradera because of the dollars his dad had sent along with him in a diplomatic pouch on the Cubana Airlines flight, but rather because of his father's revolutionary credentials, his political career, the expanding orbit of his attributes.

After breakfast, he would read a bit at the iron table from a coverless copy of Asimov's *Foundation and Empire* which Bengoa had brought, and a half-hour later he'd be in the water again. Arms spread like a cross, his back to the edge of the pool, he would bicycle his legs and watch how the hospital awoke little by little, how the ill would emerge from their rooms with lazy eyes and feet. He amused himself by thinking that the hotel was an old movie he was projecting with the movements of his legs underwater, and he would slow the bicycle down as if it was a crank that would make the scenes go by in slow motion. He always achieved the desired effect; it was a simple trick, since everyone in La Pradera moved as slow as hell.

If it was really sunny the pool would fill up by about ten a.m. and Argenis would get out, afraid of contracting some strange disease, or rather another disease, because Bengoa had made him see that he was sick, that addiction was a physical condition and that he was there to cure it. He would be cured of shooting up, although addiction itself had no cure. "Your brain will always have that hunger, that thirst for relief," Bengoa had said, as he handed Argenis a pack of Popular cigarettes.

Bengoa and Argenis had lunch together every day and they would smoke at the iron table before and after the meal, observing the staff giving a blond boy with Down syndrome water therapy. They would discuss Argenis's symptoms and then the doctor would return to the gravitational center of all his conversations, the Cuban Revolution. Bengoa had been in the mountains with Fidel and had met Argenis's father during the Latin American Solidarity Conference of

1967. He would speak of these events with the solemnity of a preacher, highlighting dates and the names of forgotten places where he'd cured the wounds, fevers, infections, and asthma of the revolutionaries' flesh. Each day Bengoa would extract a sample from his bottomless sack of anecdotes. Most of these memories were as precise as Argenis's dose of buprenorphine, and it was obvious that they filled the doctor with the same kind of calm that the medicine gave his patient. Remembering these events and their sensations, Bengoa's pupils would dilate, his pulse accelerate, and then the inevitable comedown would make him stare at the pool water and throw out a last, usually tragic, line to ease his forced landing just a bit.

"When your dad came I met Caamaño, who was training here so that he could sacrifice himself in the DR later on."

Argenis imagined the word "sacrifice" beating in Caamaño's veins and those of his companions, the dark euphoria that had made them disembark on a boggy beach on the Dominican Republic's north coast in 1973 in order to topple Balaguer's government with just nine men. A tremendous high. Cuba and its revolution had pricked their veins and those of millions of young people around the world.

When Bengoa finished his daily historical venting, it was usually just before four p.m., the time when, without fail, he would inject Argenis in his room. He could have done it by the pool, but Argenis preferred to lie down on the bed for a bit, looking at the ceiling fan or at a transfer of an Argentine flag someone had stuck onto the sliding door. Argenis had thought the flag was an allusion to Che Guevara, but Bengoa explained proudly that Maradona had once stayed in that clinic and pointed out the sticker as irrefutable proof of the star's past presence. The sticker had started to peel off and air pollution had tinted the transparent edges the same amber color as the Temgesic capsules.

Argenis had never been good at packing suitcases, which might seem strange for a professional painter with a fine arts education and a proven talent for composition, perspective, and proportion. For him, transferring objects from the world or from his imagination onto canvas in a balanced way had always been a natural inclination, even before his artistic training. When he was little he would draw his classmates' heads during the Spanish class he hated, achieving a realism so effective that his mom raced to sign him up for lessons with the master painter Silvano Lora. Silvano had been one of his parents' comrades in arms in the seventies and his exile during Balaguer's twelve years in power had been one of the topics of the article for which the journalist Orlando Martínez had been assassinated. "Orlando Martínez died so that people like you and Silvano could be free today," Etelvina had told him as they were waiting for Silvano to open the door of his studio.

Like Bengoa, Argenis's mom was a natural-born storyteller, but unlike the doctor, her memories of that era brought her little comfort. Instead they made her speak slowly and painfully, in the rhythm of someone drinking a bitter tonic.

Order and cleanliness were the only weaknesses Argenis had been able to detect in his mother. The last time she had taken him into her house, after his divorce from Mirta, he had dared to say that her desire for pulchritude was merely a Trujillist relic. Etelvina refused to speak to him for three years – until the night when, having dragged Argenis out of his pusher's apartment by force, José Alfredo had left him in her house. She had made him swallow a sedative without water and he'd awoken on her sofa twelve hours later with his stomach turning from the smell of salami being fried up for breakfast. There were two red fabric suitcases open in the middle of the living room which Etelvina was filling with clothing, tins of food, and toiletries. "Where are you going?" Argenis asked, and she looked at him, glad to see him awake, wearing an expression of tenderness he hadn't seen on her face since he was a boy.

Just hours before Bengoa picked Argenis up from La Pradera to take him to the apartment he'd rented for him in Havana's Chinatown, Argenis's clothes, which had arrived in Cuba as orderly as a good game of Tetris, had been strewn all around the room: on the bed, on the floor, falling out of drawers, and untidily hung over the towel rod in the bathroom. He was too lazy to pick them up. He was too lazy for anything. He was wearing the same old pink rubber flip-flops from his pusher's house. His new shoes, leather moccasins and a pair of sneakers, were still in one of the suitcases. The second suitcase, which contained cans of food and Nesquik, was still locked.

Argenis's grandmother Consuelo, his father's mom, had folded many more shirts and pants than Etelvina had, and not for her good-for-nothing kids, but because she had worked as a servant for more than forty years. Reflecting on those numbers, Argenis decided to fold a few items in her honor. He gathered up his things and threw them on the bed, but as he looked at the pile of dirty clothes he saw his grandmother as the Little Prince on a tiny planet of stinking clothing and dirty dishes, fighting against other people's grease, her eternal baobab. The apathy came over him again, a profound feeling of sloth, a tiredness of the world in general. "My grandmother has folded enough clothes," he thought, as if the old woman's years of hard work had exonerated him from doing the same. That exoneration, bought with Argenis's grandmother's sweat, was the excuse he used for spending every day he was married to Mirta watching porn on the internet and snorting coke, then his preferred drug, while his now ex-wife put in her nine-to-five in the Banco Hipotecario.

Argenis felt for the pack of cigarettes in his pants pocket. That rectangular bulge in his jeans calmed him a bit. He rolled everything into a big ball and stuffed it into the suitcase, pulled the zipper up with some difficulty, and went outside to smoke a Popular. It was not yet ten a.m., and after three weeks of treatment the mornings were often pitted by brief yet recurrent feelings of unease which Argenis calmed by silently repeating, "Bengoa will be here soon." If he had been under the effects of Temgesic, he'd at least have folded a shirt or two. Temgesic makes everything interesting, even dirty clothes.

Bengoa arrived and Argenis noticed that he wasn't wearing the little fanny pack with the syringes, cotton, alcohol, rubber, and vials. By way of a greeting, Argenis nervously asked, "Is the treatment already over, *asere*?" With a half-smile, the doctor wheeled his cases toward the car under a sun that made his bald head glisten and answered, "Now that you're going to have your own place, you'll be injecting yourself." When they got to the car, he handed over a box filled with twelve 3mg vials, and Argenis couldn't remember ever having been so happy in his whole life.

On their drive, Havana was looking glorious and desperate, an old woman with legs open, brazenly displaying her wide and empty streets – streets that reminded Argenis of an amusement park; no cars, buses, or trams. The people who were coming and going wore an anguish on their faces he could recognize as his own: it was the anguish of having to hustle for everything on the black market, just as he'd hustled for heroin in Santo Domingo.

The routine at La Pradera had been good for him. He felt strong and self-sufficient. "This is a new era," he told himself. As he helped to take the suitcases out of the trunk, he was conscious of the eight pounds of muscle mass he'd gained thanks to Bengoa's attentions. The renewed capabilities of his body surprised him as they carried the bags upstairs together. As if going through a second puberty, his insides swelled with something resembling the awkward happiness he'd felt when his childish cheeks were newly populated with dark hairs.

The uneven beard that had started to grow when he was thirteen was his first triumph over his brother Ernesto, who at fifteen already had two definite callings: kissing their dad's ass and making Argenis's life impossible. Ernesto was the best student in his year, besides being class president, and he had already had a couple of girlfriends. But that summer, while Argenis stood in front of the bathroom mirror trying out shaving with his mother – since José Alfredo had already left them for Genoveva – his older brother's hairless white face was colonized by the nastiest acne case in history. Traces of blood and pus stained every pillow in the house.

Their father had boasted a splendid beard from a young age. He proudly pointed it out whenever he showed them pictures from his militant stage: pictures of him at protests sporting an untrimmed Afro and thick-rimmed sunglasses. He was a different person back then, a person who knew less than Argenis did about the dark phenomena that would turn him into the hypertensive, clean-shaven, permanently suited guy who defended his party, the Dominican Liberation Party, in the newspapers.

The paint on the stairs going up to Argenis's new home was surrendering to the extreme humidity. Flakes of it hung down like the petals of an enormous funeral flower. The bronze spiral bannister decorated in art nouveau motifs had been recently polished, although here and there pieces had been hacked off by some thief or other. When they reached the fifth floor, his T-shirt soaking wet, Argenis felt like a man again and not like the shadow that had loomed over the untidy property of his best friends for the last few months.

From the apartment's entryway you could see a balcony about three meters long, and a lovely breeze was blowing in from it. He dropped his bags and walked over to see if the view of decrepit buildings, rooftops, and laundry lines had the same contagious harmony as the rest of Havana. It wasn't his first time in the city. In 1992 he had come to a summer camp for young revolutionaries from all over Latin America. His impression then had been the same as now: a heartbreaking mix of need and beauty. Standing out on the apartment's balcony, he felt like a humble eighth note in a grandiose symphony whose sounds, audible only to the soul, greatly surpassed the appearance of its score of colonial architecture, dirty water, and ideology.

Standing with him on the balcony, Bengoa was speechifying on the history of the neighborhood, on Chinese immigration, on the old folk who used to stand in their doorways smoking opium – stories that he would embellish when he felt they were too short in the telling. Then he drew a little map of the best restaurants, in case Argenis wanted to blow the twenty bucks he was going to leave him, and Argenis supposed that, just as he had considered it appropriate to trust him with the administration of his own medicine, the doctor would eventually let him manage the money his dad sent, too.

Bengoa had equipped the kitchen with coffee, sugar, bread, eggs, rice, and a couple of potatoes, stuff he pointed out while opening the cabinets with the smiling gestures of a magician showing the inside of a box in which his assistant has been pierced by swords. Then he showed him the apartment's two bedrooms, and Argenis mentally converted one of them into a painting studio. He saw himself there looking robust and inspired, putting the finishing touches to a monochromatic nude of a headless woman.

"Can I trust you?" Bengoa asked, passing him a key chain sporting a cheap medal of the Virgen de la Caridad del Cobre, and Argenis said yes, of course.

With difficulty, Argenis waited for four p.m., the time the doctor had indicated he should inject himself. To deal with the anxiety, he eyed the vial that was lying on the decorative flowers of the rattan sofa in the living room, smoked a Popular, and drank the coffee he had made in the blue *greca* pot that came with the kitchen. The coffee came from one of the five packages of Café Santo Domingo that Etelvina had put in the suitcase. Each time he saw them he loudly asked, "Why didn't you also pack me five cartons of Marlboro Lights?" as if his mother could hear him.

When only a few minutes remained, he sat down on the rattan sofa and laid all his instruments out on the coffee table. It was all much easier now that there was nothing to light. He put the needle into the vial and filled the syringe.

Bengoa hadn't left him the rubber strap, so he took off his belt, and as he tied it around his bicep the Janet Jackson song "Escapade" emerged from some place in the building. Its first notes, in this setting strange and at the same time familiar, made Argenis think about the Cubans' obsession with eighties' synthesizers, those bland keyboards that for them are the essence of modernity, the things with which Phil Collins and Peter Gabriel made millions.

Millions.

With the relief the injection brought, he savored the idea for the first time. If he had millions, he would buy all the heroin he'd need for the rest of his life. The purest goddamn smack in the world. He would live a tranquil life, not bothering anyone, disciplined and satisfied with his daily ration of happiness, as triumphant as a worker on a Soviet poster, a syringe in one fist and a giant spoon in the other.

The Bible says that God saw man was lonely, so he made him a woman from his own flesh. Argenis's father, lacking such superpowers, sent him a boom box with a CD player. Bengoa brought it over, and Susana with it, "to clean your apartment." Susana had curly dark brown hair, a perfect belly button, and beautiful toes with pink polish peeking through her plastic sandals. She had brought a cheap cloth apron, which she put on immediately in order to attack the dirty dishes piled up in the sink. The water made refreshing sounds as it splashed on the plates, though Bengoa insisted on interrupting them with his praise of Sony, the makers of the boom box.

"This is what I call aerodynamic design, Argenis. If you don't want it, I'll take it," he said with childlike enthusiasm as he plugged the apparatus in and stuck his hand without permission into the Case Logic, which was lying on the counter. He rooted around until he found a CD by Joan Manuel Serrat that Argenis never played but which the doctor apparently loved. Then he sat on one of the rocking chairs and took a swig from the flask of Havana Club he always had in his back pocket, and which he'd sometimes used to spike their coffees at La Pradera.

Susana was cleaning Argenis's room with a broom and a mop she had found in the kitchen. He could hear her clanking around in the closet and prayed she wouldn't find any dirty underwear that hadn't made it to the laundry basket. Bengoa, now standing in front of Argenis, took another swig from his bottle, grimaced, and then puckered his lips as for a kiss, looked toward the room where Susana was working and, while pushing his fat middle finger in and out of the circle he'd made with his other hand, said loudly enough for Susana to hear, "Susana studied art history, Argenis. You'll get along very well."

Later, when Susana came out to clean the living room, the two men moved onto the balcony so she could finish. Bengoa was humming along to Serrat, and Argenis, feeling a mix of arousal and annoyance, was quiet until they both left. After checking from the balcony that both of them had gotten into the Lada, he turned off the Serrat, ran to the bathroom, and lowered his pants to inspect the modest erection the episode had given him.

Thanks to the heroin he had spent many months without any desire for sex, and he was happy to see that, in spite of the Temgesic, his penis was returning to life. He touched himself to test the hardness of this rebirth and then jacked off – simply, nothing fancy. After he came he got into the shower, but there wasn't any water. Susana's cleaning had used up the contents of the rooftop tank. He put his jeans on to go up to the rooftop and look it over, see if he might at least get enough to fill a plastic jug to throw over himself. The tank was enormous, metal, homemade, and painted in red and white. When the water got low you had to fill it up with a pump you connected to the water main in the street. In Cuba, everything required a major operation. "You do it at night," Bengoa had told him. "Vantroi, your neighbor, has the pump."

Văn Trỗi. Argenis had heard that name for the first time during a Holy Week vacation at the beach house belonging to Tony Catrain, his father's best friend. He and his brother were maybe eight and ten, and Ernesto was playing a game with his father that they called "Revolutionary Dictionary." José Alfredo had made him memorize a communist hero for each letter of the alphabet and at any time and any place he might say a letter to Ernesto, who would respond like a dog hoping for a biscuit. "Nguyễn Văn Trỗi, fighter in the National Liberation Front of Vietnam," Ernesto had said that afternoon, standing out of respect, as his father had demanded, since almost every person he had had to bottle up in his mind was dead. Ernesto said it beautifully, against a picture-postcard orange sunset, but José Alfredo was waiting for the next paragraph about the fighter and Ernesto couldn't recall it. José Alfredo had been drinking with his friends all day, and he said, "This boy is such a shit. He always makes me look bad."

Văn Trỗi had been captured as he placed explosives on a bridge that was soon to be crossed by McNamara, U.S. Secretary of Defense. After months of torture, they finally shot him on 15 October 1964. Argenis never forgot that fact, because later that night, as they were getting into the tent Tony Catrain had fixed up in the living room for his son Charlie, Argenis, and Ernesto, Ernesto kept repeating it as though he were praying to scare off a monster.

How many children had been named for figures in his father's and Ernesto's dictionary? How many knew the stories behind them? Did they care? Had any of them honored their memories with a warlike act, with the pursuit of an ideal, with a revolutionary deed? Those children, marked by their parents' ideological passion, who were they now?

The polished bricks of the rooftop's floor, with its little pink cement stage in the middle, added color to a picturesque scene in which the water tank, which resembled the shell of a Soviet rocket, was the star. A pair of prize-worthy legs crowned with extremely short jean shorts was stood on a wooden crate, so that their owner could peer through the hole at the top of the tank. They were the legs of a six-ties Italian actress, just rounded enough yet still far from Rubenesque. Only the calf, thanks to the high-heeled clogs, displayed a timid muscle that directed the gaze down a pleas-ing slope to the ankle. The comrade's torso was wrestling inside the tank like an alien with the stalled motor of its spaceship, and the struggle was such that at times her feet came off the box that supported them and hung in the air. Without warning she removed her torso, arms, and head from inside, spattering water about and gasping for air with an open mouth. A kind of hook was in her right hand, but it was no she – it was a lanky mulatto guy. He had no shirt on and was wiping the excess water from his ripped pecs with his hands, which sported long, fake, purple nails. His back was that of a welterweight boxer and, seen in this context, his shaved legs completed the ensemble. "I fixed the tank, niño. I'm Vantroi, your neighbor," he said. Argenis made an effort to put his hand into the one Vantroi extended to him, and Vantroi shook it with a coarse virility that was in perfect harmony with the tough appearance of his clogs' heels.

When at last he was under the shower, washing away the traces of masturbation, of Vantroi, and of the Havana heat, the brief uneasiness that preceded his daily dose intensified. The echo of the conflicting halves of his neighbor's body, Bengoa's alcohol-fueled gestures, the incessant yelling that came from behind the miserable walls, and his own recent history reached a fatal level, as if someone had suddenly cranked up the volume on negativity. He emerged from the bathroom drying himself nervously, thinking about how bad his mother must have felt when she saw him that morning stinking of shit, unshaven, and incoherent. His heart was racing and he threw himself on the bed with his eyes closed, as if this could stop the images of the past three years of his life from sloshing over him, like crap in a toilet. He opened his eyes and a widened field of vision now included a Quaker Oats calendar that had been tacked up next to a poster of Che Guevara on the closet door. Seen together there, Che's face – the same one plastered onto hats and stickers all over the world – and the happy Quaker were the two sides of a grotesque yin-yang, on the one hand a socialist ideal turned into merchandise and on the other a contraband capitalist brand that sustained the biological functioning of the revolution against all odds.

The previous months' pages had been torn from the calendar, and the days of April 2004, the month in progress, stood out from the background, orange against dark blue. In a few weeks there would be elections in the Dominican Republic and according to all the polls his father's party, the PLD, was going to win again. Until that moment he hadn't asked himself why his father was trying harder than ever before to care for him, even if it was in Cuba and through Bengoa. It didn't take long to reach the obvious yet painful conclusion that José Alfredo had sent him to Havana less out of concern for his son's mental health than for the health of his own political career. A junkie son is a gift from heaven for anyone engaged in a dirty campaign, the kind of campaign that got dirtier the closer it got to the election. His father had freed himself of his problem and at the same time he had, in the eyes of the world, done a good deed for his son. On his way to the living room, Argenis, still naked, spit on the poster of Che as if it were José Alfredo's face. "You're a son of a bitch, but I'm an even bigger son of a bitch. You put me here because you're ashamed of me, but I'm doing just fine with your money, cocksucker." He took out two Temgesic vials instead of one and mentally rehearsed an excuse for Bengoa: "I needed something stronger, I had a panic attack." He filled the syringe completely with 6mg of the stuff and shot up, contentedly imagining his mom and dad watching him through a peephole and seeing how his eyes rolled with pleasure on his way to the stratosphere.

He still couldn't motivate himself to go outside. Everything that happened on the other side of his apartment door seemed menacing and strange. He preferred to read *Foundation and Empire*, the Asimov book Bengoa had loaned him, to listen to his CDs, and to limit his outings to the balcony, where he'd lean out like an old gossip for hours, watching the confident comings and goings of others. There, he learned the intimate rhythms of his neighborhood: its rush hours, its secrets, the catalog of tonalities the light extracted from all things. The street bubbled over like a pressure cooker, full of unfamiliar gestures, of struggles and issues, of small aggressions, of possibility, of events Argenis pretended he could calculate before confronting them. Everything he needed, Bengoa brought. His little zone of control and its small disasters – power outages or water shortages, things also common in Santo Domingo – made him feel secure and calm.

For the first week, he shut himself in the bedroom he didn't use for sleeping, put Lou Reed on the boom box, sat on the floor and, in his mind, converted the space into an extraordinary studio. It was really Philip Guston's studio, which he'd seen in a documentary, although it was his own paint dripping down the canvases in the imaginary workshop. There were unpainted and half-finished works all over the place. On top of a large metal-topped wooden table were several plastic buckets full of brushes, some soaking in water and others brand new, with their bristles pointing up. They were good brushes, like the ones his father had bought on his trip to France with Genoveva to congratulate Argenis on getting into the Altos de Chavón art school. Mirta must have thrown those brushes out, he thought, because he'd never gone back to collect them after the divorce. The table had a shelf below it full of cans of acrylic paint, like the ones Guston used. Strange and mistreated objects from other eras, the kind he used to buy in Little Haiti behind the Mercado Modelo in Santo Domingo, adorned the corners. When the room was ready, he lit a Popular on this side of reality and, eyes closed, contemplated the piece he was working on in that magnificent place. The air smelled of paint, sweat, piles of cigarette butts, and the soot of the street.

I have to be careful with this, he thought one morning. I can't let things end up the way they did with the grant.

Three years ago he had received a grant from some gallery owners on the north coast. All he had to do was paint and accept the advice of a famous curator who had been contracted to guide him and two other Dominican artists along the ambiguous path of contemporary art. Argenis had just gotten divorced and was trying to give up cocaine. Still immature, he thought he was the next Goya. He started playing around with the idea that in another life he had been a buccaneer. He imagined his days in that life, with ample details, and then painted them. It was a very intense and attractive process, but what began as a creative game ended as a psychotic breakdown, and he was committed to the mental health wing of the UCE for several weeks. Not even his mother had come to see him, and he didn't blame her. Back then she was fed up with his nonsense, his insomnia, his obsessions. Argenis couldn't make anything work, despite not wanting for opportunities. He hadn't been born on a sugarcane plantation like his father, nor had they confiscated his paintings, tortured, and deported him, as had happened with half of his parents' friends in the seventies. What the hell was wrong with him?

The second time Susana came to clean, she came alone, and Bengoa sent twelve vials of Temgesic along with her. Argenis didn't know if he'd done it out of negligence or an excess of confidence, because he'd only been in the apartment for a week and he was supposed to take one a day. In any case, it was perfect. He'd been taking the double dose for a couple of days and had only two left, which with the twelve Susana brought added up to the fourteen needed to square off the happy weekly mathematics of his consumption.

It was about ten a.m. and he was still in bed, since the dose from the day before had helped him to sleep late. Susana had a copy of Bengoa's key, and she peeked into the bedroom with a bucket in her hand. Argenis had just gotten up, having heard the front door open, and he rubbed his eyes with an intense feeling of grogginess. "Good morning, Mr. Luna," she said, and he told her to call him Argenis as he scratched his balls on his way to the bathroom and breathed in the baby cologne she used by way of perfume.

"You want coffee?" she asked from the kitchen, and he remembered the coffees his ex-wife Mirta had brought him years ago before she left for work in the morning. They had agreed that while she was working he would prepare his first solo show. Instead he would snort a half gram of coke while watching videos of black men with barely legal white women and make a few scribbles in a sketch book an hour before she came home, just to have something to show her – the sketches for a supposed future "monumental" piece.

Susana served her overly sweet Cuban coffee on the balcony in old porcelain cups, along with some toast Argenis smeared with the Maggi mayonnaise his mother had bestowed upon his luggage. They spoke of his parents, his brother Ernesto, his studies at the School of Fine Arts. She listened with interest, not saying anything until – since Bengoa had told him she'd studied art history – Argenis asked who her favorite artist was. "Of all time?" she asked nervously, as if her response could save her life, and then said "Goya" without moving her eyes from the toast she was eating, and without him moving his from her orange-flecked lips, from the clavicles split by the narrow straps of her top, from the feet whose shoes had been left by the front door. That day, he helped her make the bed and wash the dishes, and when it was time for lunch he delved into his suitcase to share a can of beans with her, opening it as if it were a bottle of champagne. When it was time for her to leave, a time that coincided with that of his injection, Susana pulled a little book from her wrinkly fake leather purse and put it in his hand. "It's a gift for you, Argenis." It was a guide to the collection of the Hermitage Museum, in Russian and with a very dilapidated cover. She left before he could thank her, and as he listened to her footsteps going down the stairs, his heart crumpled in his chest like a rejected sketch in the hand of its draftsman.

Sitting on his bed preparing the syringe, he watched through the window as a woman in the next building hung up clothing in her bedroom. Pink pants, a blouse, athletic socks. Things acquired a distinct thickness in the few seconds preceding the injection. The intense anticipation melted down material objects and their subatomic reality became evident: the orange blouse and the woman's hand were made of the same stuff – uncertain particles, the ideas of things. He thought of all the trouble monks went to, in order to feel something similar. In the stupor of the first few hours of his high, he paged through Susana's booklet as if a secret message was hiding in those pages, a message he'd have to decipher. After plenty of speculation he closed the gift, noticed the dirt under his fingernails and went to the bathroom to clean them with a toothbrush and a drop of shampoo. When they were done he shaved the beard he hadn't trimmed since getting to Chinatown, and then did the same with the hair on his head. He was wearing it in a short Afro that he first had to trim down with a little pair of scissors his mother had put into a transparent plastic bag, along with other toiletries. Then he shaved his head completely, nicking himself a few times. As he went over the back of his neck with the green plastic Bic razor, he felt something like the pleasure his mother must have felt, imagining him regularly using those implements. He washed off the specks of blood and doused his head and face in Old Spice aftershave, his father's favorite.

All that shaving business in the windowless bathroom had made him sweat, and he decided to shower. The water was cold and he counted to three and closed his eyes before taking the first step. The memory of his grandmother Consuelo came to him, sitting on the bench in the kitchen where she was cleaning rice in a punch bowl, teaching him how to remove the stones, husks, and rotten grains with his fingers. Argenis opened the suitcase full of clothes – he still hadn't managed to put his things into drawers – pulled out a pair of khaki Dockers and opened a package of Fruit of the Loom undershirts. The new clothes looked good on him and smelled like they came from far away. The smell of American merchandise was a common one in Santo Domingo, but in Cuba the embargo and limited mobility had transformed that smell into a magical essence.

He went to the room he'd been imagining as his studio and placed Susana there, too, sitting on a wooden bench, her legs crossed the way he'd seen her sit. She shared a cigarette with him and he dared to get closer, to speak tenderly to her, to kiss her. This must be how Cubans dream up mental banquets, he thought, meals with appetizers, main courses, and desserts, on abundant tables made of desire. The difference was that they did it out of necessity, and Argenis did it out of cowardice. He was afraid to paint in the real world, to fail again, to go out, to be judged, to accept that he had felt something for Susana, and afraid to do anything about it.

He opened the door with his heart going a mile a minute, and went down the stairs – toward the outside, the street – in threes, at the risky speed with which children run downhill, knowing that if they fall they'll break their teeth. The night had swallowed all ugliness, and what the scarce light from isolated lampposts revealed instead was instances of sublime beauty: architectural fragments, snippets of style arranged like a collage on black cardboard.

He headed north on Campanario Street, letting himself be guided by the little neighborhood map Bengoa had made for him. Neither his simple clothes nor his sandals nor the dark skin inherited from his father gave away the still-apprehensive foreign tourist wandering the streets of Havana that night. The restaurants were to the right, but he didn't want to spend the little money he had, so he kept going.

37

He didn't know how many blocks separated him from the sea, but he shared with Cubans the certainty that, after a certain number of steps in any direction, you will always find a shore.

His throat quickly filled with the particles of salt that traveled on the wind. When he came to Virtudes Street he thought he could hear the slap of the waves against the cliffs, but it was only the rumbling of a black Buick hidden in the shadows. Its owner was trying to get it to start, holding a flashlight between his teeth. There were no children, nor any businesses in sight. Leaning against the frames, a few shirtless men peered from darkened doorways while the laughter of old folks, Latin pop music, and a vague smell of cooking oil emanated from other doorways lit up by electric light and conversation.

The feel of salt in the breeze intensified to the point of dampening his shirt, his arm hair and his cheeks. The Atlantic placed its hand on him like a delicate lover, pulling him toward the street by the sea, the Malecón, toward the ends of the earth. When he arrived, he saw several couples sitting on the wall and sharing long kisses, always followed by a whispered secret or the meeting of foreheads, while on the other side of the wall, on the reef, a big-bellied man was fishing with a string tied to his index finger.

He felt like he was in his element. He felt, at least for a moment, grateful to life. Not to his father, whose attentions were always subtitled, but rather to life itself and to the opportunity he thought he still had, to free himself definitively from his opiate dependence. When would the treatment be over? He ought to ask Bengoa. Did Susana know he was an addict? What was her relationship to the doctor? Did she have a boyfriend? What did her relatives do? Did he have a shot with her? Question after question spilled from his guts with all the persistence of the waves' ebb and flow. All of a sudden there were so many of them and they were so unending that he felt dizzy. He lay on the wall looking up and watched how the wind erased the clouds from the sky to leave a flaming yellow moon in its center.

Susana would return in a few days, Argenis supposed, so in the meantime he naturally fell into a pleasant routine that made the waiting a little easier. After a breakfast of coffee and toast with mayonnaise, he would go out for a walk with the Asimov book in the back pocket of his jeans. It was an old paperback edition and he had to be careful when he pulled it out, so as not to drop any loose pages. The ad-free walls and signposts on the way to the Malecón surprised him. Aside from the government's anachronistic propaganda, Havana was a naked city. The painted slogans and heroes found here and there seemed as rustic and naive as the tattoos etched by hand onto the arms and backs of prisoners. Although the paint was almost always recent and often even fresh, you could see from their outlines that the designs were old and the brushes had only been there to touch them up.

He wondered whether the unflagging permanence of those signs was inversely proportional to the faith people still put in them. What would his father, the José Alfredo Luna of today, think about all this? Time had extracted those slogans from his mouth like decaying molars, replacing them with the good teeth he and his party friends used to consume lobster and Black Label on a daily basis. When Argenis was little, his father had used those slogans to complete his thoughts and as greetings. Che Guevara's

40

"Hasta la victoria, siempre!" was his favorite. As well as the Revolutionary Dictionary, he had made Ernesto memorize Che's farewell letter to Fidel, which was the source of that phrase, his most famous one. His brother would recite it with a practiced fervor, with which he milked his parents for years. José Alfredo didn't have time to teach Argenis these things, nor did Argenis want to learn them. They seemed as boring, mysterious, and as completely foreign to him as the prayers to Archangel San Miguel his grandmother Consuelo would sing as she rested her hands on his head. Both were liturgies from a distant planet.

He knew he was an illiterate in the strange communist atmosphere. He took slow baby steps across the ideological surface, interested mainly in its effects on people – the small obsessions, the oblique explosions of silent desperation in their eyes.

Years before, when he was still pursuing a career as an artist, he had hated what he called "Cuban opportunism." In his opinion the revolution and the U.S. embargo that followed were interesting issues that Cubans exploited as artists, issues that gave them an edge, and he considered the ease with which they could petition for political asylum an injustice, the networks they created to publicize and distribute their work when they managed to leave Cuba a mafia. But these inventions were really the product of his envy, since Havana was and still is the one and only New York of the Caribbean, the Paris of the Antilles, the New Delhi of the West Indies. Envy ate him alive: he envied their delicious eloquence, their Wifredo Lams and Gutiérrez Aleas, their Lecuonas and their Alejo Carpentiers. He even envied them their hunger and their suffering.

On some streets, after he had stopped multiple times to ask directions on his morning walk, people began to recognize him. His Dominican accent was funny to them. "You sound like you're from Oriente," they'd say, and he knew that they thought people "from Oriente" spoke as bad as all fuck. In spite of their economic hardship, people still had enough energy to put on the reggaeton, *balada*, or salsa music that poured from houses at the pathological volume used for listening to such things in the Caribbean.

Sitting on the Malecón, he would read a few pages of his disintegrating book until a high-school escapee would pull his attention away from it and toward her shapely legs and girlish shoes, or until the breeze would snatch a page from his negligent hands and he'd have to run a few meters to reach it. Then he would walk to Galiano Street and, after resting a few minutes in front of the Bellevue Hotel, walk the ten blocks back southwards to Chinatown.

He always arrived home dying of hunger, and then he'd put on a Cream CD while he prepared the cup of white rice he'd eat with ketchup. He'd drink another coffee, smoke a Popular, and, sitting on the living room sofa as he waited the last few hours until his injection, he'd plan his outings with Susana, choose the songs he'd play for her, deliberate which Chinese restaurant in the neighborhood he should take her to, even though he still hadn't been to any of them.

The plastic hand of the wall clock neared four p.m. at exactly the same time as the needle with his daily 6mg neared his arm. Under the effects of the Temgesic he needed no entertainment. Listening to an entire King Crimson album in the rocking chair on the balcony was enough to feel sated for the rest of the day. Sometimes he'd draw in his mind – fugitive lines inspired by the music, abstract objects formed by the melodies, waves that repeated to the beat of the percussion. He would miss this creative calm when drugs were definitively out of his life.

When neither Bengoa nor the medicine nor Susana had appeared by the seventh day after her previous visit, the landscape of Argenis's placid routine filled with black clouds. He had one dose left, which is to say two vials of Temgesic, and on the other side of their consumption lay only the awful abyss. He wasn't familiar with the ill effects of abstaining from Temgesic, but because of the similarities between the two drugs he imagined they'd be similar to those of heroin. He understood that Bengoa had given him the extra vials in case he couldn't come, and Argenis, of course, had used all of them. He prayed for Bengoa's return with an intense but disposable faith, the kind he always had when he knew he was fucked. He jabbed the needle in nervously, hurting himself a bit in the process, but not even the enforced tranquility of the chemical could settle his insides. Bengoa had left a number to call if anything was wrong, but he'd have to borrow a neighbor's phone and he didn't know how to explain to the doctor that he'd upped his dosage without asking.

Maybe this was his big opportunity. To quit Temgesic. Get clean. Suffer the withdrawal symptoms like a real macho. He wasn't addicted to heroin anymore, but it was clear that a hand just as strong was now clenched around his will. Maybe he could get Temgesic on the street. Maybe if there wasn't any Temgesic, he could get a little heroin. He had twenty bucks and a lot of experience asking strange questions in bad neighborhoods. He could already see himself heating up the spoon with blameless pleasure. Maybe it was destiny. After all, he'd never wanted to give up heroin. They had kidnapped him, made him do it. He was ready to go and ride it out, he was standing by the door, but then he saw the bottle of ketchup Etelvina had put in his suitcase, the one he used to flavor his lunches of plain rice, standing on the kitchen table.

When Argenis was little, that red sauce was the only thing that could get him to eat. It was the camouflage his mother used to hide the flavor of eggs, plantains, cabbage, beans. Back then he was a restless skeleton with a closed stomach, a kid who only really liked to eat sausage links and drink Nesquik. His brother Ernesto had their father's appetite, and whenever Etelvina gave up on Argenis she would add his eternal and abundant leftovers to Ernesto's plate.

The smell of his mother's apartment in Santo Domingo reached all the way to Havana. It was the smell of a kitchen always in use, the smell of her students' uncorrected papers, and the smell of Anaïs Anaïs she sprayed over her clothing before leaving for work. Like a red ink pen, the Baldom ketchup bottle had drawn a line straight back to those years, just before his parents' divorce, when Etelvina was working like a dog both in and out of the house in order to pay the bills for Argenis, Ernesto, and José Alfredo, who was just about to take off with Genoveva.

Argenis felt in his bones the tiredness that his mother had felt on those afternoons, scrubbing the dishes with dark sweat stains in the armpits of her tailored suits. Back then he always spat those dinners back out onto his plate, the dinners she'd come all the way back home to make, riding there in a stinking *concho* in the break between two classes at the university. Something akin to empathy, sadness, or responsibility overwhelmed him and he realized that his mother had extended her sphere of influence to touch him through the squeezy ketchup bottle she'd put in his luggage. She had injected him with some of her patience, the same patience she'd pulled out from under some rock back then so she wouldn't shoot herself in the head. He decided to wait until the next day to make any decision, and instead spent the afternoon on the balcony finishing the Asimov book, which that piece of shit had ended on a cliffhanger so you'd have to buy the next one.

"*Asere*, this is communism. You think I get those vials from a bottomless tank?" Bengoa was on his knees, complaining about the mistake Argenis had made, about the extra Temgesics he'd consumed, about the trouble this would make for him, as he searched the kitchen trash bag for the used syringes and empty vials that would confirm the details of Argenis's confession.

All this was pretty far from his stupid plans with Susana, who was cleaning the kitchen, eyes on the floor, while the doctor scolded him. If she didn't already know it, Bengoa had now made it clear to her. Argenis was a junkie. A big, fat junkie. Such a junkie that he had gotten hooked on the medicine meant to detox him. As if that weren't enough, when Bengoa saw Argenis fiddling with the sugar bowl on the kitchen table, head hanging, the doctor changed his tone and spoke to him as if he were a child: "Argenis, son, you have to take advantage of this opportunity. Think of your dad, spending all this money on you. You can't let him down." Argenis considered telling him what he thought of his father, but it wouldn't have helped him any. He wanted the doctor to leave, but he also didn't want to be left alone with Susana. "From now on you'll have to come to my house for your injections, every afternoon at four." He left him the two vials for that day and put the ones he'd brought

46

with him back into his fanny pack. He pointed out a bag of oatmeal, powdered milk, and cabbage he'd brought and said, "Tell Susana to draw you a map to my house," before taking off without saying goodbye or leaving any money.

As soon as Bengoa was gone, Susana stuck her head out of the kitchen and said, "Don't pay any mind to that asshole." With a knitted brow she rummaged through the bag the doctor had brought, as if it were full of shit. "They're paying him to take care of you, Argenis, not to shame you." When she tossed the bag and its contents onto the table she didn't look anything like the person who had run downstairs, smiling, after giving him the book the week before. "What is it you feel when you use it? What is it about it that you like?" she asked. No one who wasn't an addict had ever asked him that. "I feel good," Argenis said. "When I shoot up I don't need anything else." She had no advice, just looked at him free of judgment, as if he had told her his shirt size. Standing, she pulled her hair into a ponytail and went back to the kitchen. A few minutes later the pot whistled, and they drank the coffee with toast smeared with the peanut butter from a jar he had opened just for her. Then he put on Crosby, Stills & Nash, and she liked it almost as much as the peanut butter. She spoke to him about things she'd seen on her way there, unimportant things like the stuff his mother had told him as a kid to keep his mind off a skinned knee. Argenis examined her face in feigned tranquility, searching for a hint of contempt in her empathy. But Susana wasn't like that. She came from a reality light-years away from his, one where his addiction was just another phenomenon, and not a scandal.

As Argenis gathered up the breakfast plates, which Bengoa was paying Susana to wash with his father's money, he said he didn't want her to clean anymore today and invited her to take a walk instead. Without thinking twice, she slung her purse over her shoulder and put on her shoes. They went down the five flights in an uncomfortable silence that Argenis broke when they got to the street, to offer her a cigarette. They took the route Argenis used each day to go to the Malecón and she told him her father had gone to Florida in the Mariel boatlift and she'd never heard from him again. Susana had studied art history because she loved art but had no talent for drawing. "Neither do most contemporary artists," he said, and she laughed with her mouth open, choking a bit and throwing her head back. She stopped all of a sudden, as if something about Argenis had been revealed to her mid-laugh, then asked him, "Why don't you paint anymore?"

"Painting is over," he explained. "What people want now are Japanese toys, video loops on twenty walls, women who stick barbed wire up their asses."

The laughter returned, and then, her face serious again, Susana said, "I understand about the public, but what about the pleasure?" The pleasure of painting: the pleasure of dipping a brush, of smearing it onto the canvas, of wetting, crushing, spreading, filling, of smelling something coming to life, the physical exertion of stretching canvas across a frame.

He missed his School of Fine Arts days, when he was living in the overly hot studio across from the cathedral Etelvina had managed to convince José Alfredo to rent for him. He missed the beautiful rituals that preceded the actual painting – the trips to Chinconchan, a suffocating den of a store with rolls of paper reaching to the ceiling, the stops at the carpenter's in Santa Barbara, who'd make little frames for him from leftover pieces of wood. He missed the ice-cold beers and the stories he had shared with the old painters in the Cafetería El Conde. But most of all he missed feeling hopeful, blessed with a talent that continually manifested itself in sweaty painting sessions, always applauded by his teachers at the stultifying fine arts school. That was before he went to Altos de Chavón, the school where he learned that painting had been out of style for decades and that for many of his contemporaries it was an obsolete craft, like macramé.

"Pleasure?" Argenis repeated, playing for time, and then, as a sort of answer, he asked, "Pleasure without others?" In the face of his question, Susana made the same gesture Bengoa's cabbage and oatmeal had deserved and said, "You're the expert on that topic."

The rest of the way to the Malecón, Argenis was a whirlwind of ideas. He thought about heroin, about the paradigm of individual gratification. He had sacrificed everything – family, work, health – for it. But painting, something that had made him happy since childhood and which didn't harm anyone, terrified him. Or rather, he was terrified of doing something considered outdated. He was afraid of rejection, of being made fun of, criticized. They were the fears of a child wearing old shoes that his classmates would laugh at. While he was thinking, Susana maintained a strange silence, as if she could read the effect her words had on him, as if she had access to his mental processes and, with an invisible hand, were guiding him toward a more productive conclusion.

Before crossing the avenue to sit on the Malecón wall, he stopped to look at her. A strong wind swept some strands of hair into her face. The salt air dampened the asphalt and the walls; they breathed in iodine. A bit of hair stuck to her mouth and as she pulled it out with one hand Argenis took the opportunity to grab the other one.

There are gestures that never end, whose expanding shock waves destroy several nearby galaxies. For the few seconds it took them to cross the Malecón's six lanes, their interlaced fingers had that effect on Argenis's universe. He let go on the other side, so that the blast wouldn't kill them both, and asked if she wanted to go have an ice cream at Coppelia, as if nothing had happened. She agreed with a nod, though she was as disconcerted as he was, while hailing a cocotaxi for the two of them.

What the gesture meant or what it had done to them didn't matter. All that mattered was its power, and their desire to feel it again. They ate their ice cream at a little table much like the wrought-iron one in La Pradera. Mentioning that resemblance allowed Argenis to fill the crater their joined hands had left in the conversation with insipid facts about his hospital stay, facts he let fly without raising his eyes from the ice cream. It went down his esophagus like razor blades due to the approaching hour of his dosage, his habitual anxiety intensified by the possibility of a close encounter with Susana. He watched her put her spoon in her mouth and taste the residue on it, the bowl now empty, and he knew that he would do whatever it took to fuck her. "Shall we go?" she asked, reading his mind, and he didn't even try to bargain with the taxi driver when he asked for Argenis's last ten bucks to take them back to the apartment.

"Women with sugary cunts," the old painters in the Cafetería El Conde had called them during the conversations about art, sex, and politics they had had every day after Argenis came out of art school. "Women who turn your cock into a tongue that can taste their exquisite honey." The first time he penetrated Susana there on the kitchen table, Argenis prayed to those honorable sages, who, now that he had met that woman, had been elevated to the category of prophets.

Bengoa's house in Habana Vieja was a smallish nineteenth-century mansion whose furniture had been new in the fifties. He had hung up a few unframed still lifes by some mediocre student in the family, cheapening the neoclassic style of the home. From the living room ceiling hung a crystal chandelier from which bits of rust and flakes of paint constantly rained down. Bengoa was divorced and when his daughters weren't around dirty plates stacked up in the sink. His only efforts at cleanliness were devoted to his car and the little hair that remained on his head, which he perfumed excessively.

On his first visit, Bengoa gave Argenis a tour of his home. The living room and dining room were enormous, with fifteen-foot ceilings and floors of creole tiles in green and yellow geometric patterns. Two blue, poorly painted Ionic columns held up the arch that separated the two spaces. Another set of arch-topped columns led from the main room to another living room with a Persian rug and Arabic-style suite that sat in front of a beautiful mahogany case filled with a huge collection of classical music on vinyl. Although the LPs looked as dusty as the rest of the furnishings, Argenis guessed Bengoa did listen to them, since the record player's cover was open and inside sat a record of Beethoven's Pastoral Symphony.

A long hallway led to three bedrooms with enormous carved wooden doors Bengoa didn't bother to open. At the end was an interior courtyard leading to a separate room Bengoa called his office, which had been the servants' quarters in the house's youth.

In there, Bengoa had a desk, two folding metal chairs, a cabinet with a glass door, and a framed poster of Goya's *Saturn Devouring His Son* on the wall. It was a souvenir from the Prado, whose name was printed on its edge, which Bengoa had brought back from his only trip off the island. Argenis felt a bit dizzy and told Bengoa so, hoping he'd hurry the operation a bit. The doctor opened the cabinet with a skeleton key and pulled out two Temgesic vials. The afternoon was cool, and after the injection Bengoa invited Argenis to drink an orange juice in his courtyard next to the ruins of a stone fountain. He also proposed a game of Chinese checkers, which Argenis asked to put off to the next day, since Susana was expecting him.

On his way home, Goya's hungry Saturn alternated in his head with images from the real world, like in those movies where they crosscut the principal character's actions with fragments of some classical painting, zooming in and out to create suspense or even terror. He knew that painting like the back of his hand. What had the famous portrait of Father Time touched in him?

When he got back to his apartment, Susana was frying potatoes in the kitchen, and he told her what had happened. She took the potatoes out with a spatula and divided them equally between two plates already holding a fried egg each. As they ate, Susana told him that Goya had painted his Saturn on the wall of his dining room at the Quinta del Sordo, one of his last homes. Argenis could recall a bit about it but didn't interrupt because Susana was telling it all with such a pleasing familiarity. "In the late nineteenth century they removed it, along with the other Black Paintings, and transferred them to canvas." With her mouth full, she explained the process: "They used a very delicate glue to stick the painting from the wall onto Japanese silk paper, pulled off the layer with the picture, and transferred it onto the canvas." Her words came out naturally, but with a distinctive tone, and Argenis intuited that she hadn't read this in a book or on the internet but had received it from the lips of one of her teachers.

When Argenis was six years old, Tony Catrain, his father's best friend, had given him a book called *Myths and Legends.* It was a huge yellow hardback with delicate watercolor illustrations of the Greek and Roman gods and heroes. That book accompanied him to the School of Fine Arts, where some cocksucker stole it from him along with his lunch bag. In it he'd read the story of Kronos, Saturn to the Romans, for the first time. Like most of the ancient gods and heroes, he receives a troublesome prophecy: that one of his children will dethrone him. To avoid this fate, he eats his children as soon as they are born. His wife, made desperate by the macabre barbecue, hides their sixth child (Zeus/Jupiter) on an island and in his place gives Kronos a rock for lunch. Later, the adult Zeus, with the help of a cosmic conspiracy, gives his father a medicine that induces vomiting, and all his siblings come out again, alive and well.

Susana's mythological knowledge was less rudimentary than that of Argenis, and she described Saturn's symbolic attribute, the sickle, for him as they drank coffee on the balcony. In the background "I'm Your Captain" by Grand Funk Railroad was playing, which Argenis had put on that morning and which she had asked him to play again. "Saturn castrated his father, the Sky, with the sickle. The sickle represents time, which defines our dimension, our mastery of the planetary movements, according to which we plan our harvests here on Earth." Her words were no longer a copy of some teacher's, nor were they lines she'd memorized from a book – they were her own, improvised out of a talent for poetry that Argenis attributed not only to her personal abilities but also to the geographic coordinates of her birthplace. A few days later, he asked her to bring her things over and she showed up with a very old beige fabric suitcase, which, once emptied, he installed as decoration in the room that would someday be his studio.

During those first weeks, Argenis could feel the tiny seeds of good in him reaching up toward Susana's sun. He loved talking to her as much as he enjoyed fucking her and they did both things each morning, since in the evening, thanks to the Temgesic, his penis wasn't good for much. After sex they'd go out for a walk and Susana would fill him up with historical and aesthetic details about their surroundings, about the exuberant colonial edifices and the unfeeling revolutionary monuments, about the age of the mahogany trees, about witchcraft in wartime, the reasons for the name of a plaza or the title of a hundred-year-old piece of *son* music. Susana took a sentimental X-ray of the city and Argenis tried to make out the spots of the cancer of disillusionment on it. One day, as they prepared a plantain stew, Argenis asked, "Why don't they just kill Castro?" She went pale, as if Castro himself had overheard and was on his way to eat them alive. Sitting down on the living room sofa she said, very softly, "We don't know what to believe anymore." She sat there with watery eyes, looking at the coffee table until the stew was ready, and Argenis regretted having opened that door. He felt frivolous and ignorant, like those American tourists who say "ándale,

ándale" like Speedy Gonzales whenever they get drunk in Latin America.

After lunch, she would read him bits from Lezama Lima's *Paradiso* in bed and he would descend those motley steps into an hour-long nap. Sometimes he would dream of Santo Domingo with all its noise and trash, or that Rambo the pusher had come to Havana all dressed in red and brought him some Afghani heroin with serious balls, or that Susana had given birth to blond twins with scary-looking eyes clouded by glaucoma.

In the afternoons he'd visit Bengoa and play a round of Chinese checkers with him in the room with the vinyl records. The Beethoven LP continued to wait silently inside the record player and Argenis didn't dare ask its owner if it was because he liked it a lot or because he was too lazy to return it to its sleeve. Bengoa never made an effort to put on music. Instead he would whistle Silvio Rodríguez songs, tell dirty jokes, and confess how hard it was to support his two daughters, even as a doctor with a degree. Argenis wanted to believe he was sharing his economic woes with him to justify the fact that, beyond the rent for the apartment and the boxes of oatmeal and potatoes, he never saw a cent of the 500 dollars José Alfredo sent every month, money that Susana said would allow them to live like royalty.

One afternoon, as he returned from his appointment with Bengoa, Argenis saw his neighbor Vantroi dancing in his apartment, through the door he had left open to let some air in. The apartment was light on furniture. The only items Argenis could see were something that looked like a park bench against one wall, and a small table. In the middle of all this space in front of a twelve-inch Sony Trinitron TV connected to a VCR, Vantroi, clad in bike shorts, was copying Janet Jackson's moves in the "When I Think Of You" video.

Argenis remembered that video, made so that it would look like it had been just one take; they used to play it on Channel 2 between programs. On his feet Vantroi wore a pair of Reebok Classics, so dirty that they existed only in mummified form, thanks to countless strips of duct tape. Argenis was feeling generous after his Temgesic, and went into his place to get the turquoise-blue Adidas with orange stripes on the sides, which his mother had bought in Carrefour. He had never once worn them and they smelled fantastic. He poked his head round his neighbor's door and tossed the shoes in for him to try on.

"Who recorded the videos for you?" Argenis asked, since he knew there was no MTV in Cuba, and Vantroi answered, "Juani, my cousin in Chicago," as he moved his feet along with the video, staring down at the Adidas. Without stopping the rhythmic movements of his shoulders and head, he came over to the door to tell Argenis, "I just really admire Paula Abdul's work as a choreographer," and added, still following exactly what was happening in the video, "that mix of jazz and street."

At dinner, when she'd learned of Argenis's extreme solidarity, Susana looked at him with a mix of tenderness and disapproval, and then asked if he had told either Bengoa or his father to give him the 500 dollars directly. Argenis said no, that he was waiting for the right moment. In fact, he had had no contact at all with his father aside from a signed photo José Alfredo had sent of himself with the newly elected president, and he felt a bit bad about firing Bengoa from his most lucrative side job. The next morning, as she bounced up and down on his balls, Susana made him promise her that he would talk to Bengoa about the 500 bucks that afternoon, moaning as she asked. Argenis came inside her to seal his promise and after a cold shower and a good lunch, he put on a button-down shirt with the khaki pants and leather moccasins his mother had chosen, in case some special occasion ever presented itself in Cuba. Susana kissed him before he left, something Mirta had never done, and he went down the stairs like a proud provider.

Bengoa greeted him affectionately, complimented his clothing, and told Argenis that the care he'd put into dressing was a sign of health. "You're as good as new," Bengoa told him on the way to his office, where he always performed the injection in front of Saturn. Argenis got nervous during the checkers game and Bengoa offered him a Popular and a swig of his Havana Club. He wet his mouth with the rum and waited to finish the cigarette before telling the doctor they had to discuss something. "What's up, Argenis? Is Susana not doing a good job?" "It isn't that," he said. "It's just that I think I can manage my own money." Bengoa got serious, and put the yellow marble he was holding down onto the board at random, ending the game.

"What money are you talking about, Argenis?" the doctor asked with his head at an angle, like a dog trying to understand human speech, and Argenis explained he was talking about the money his father sent every month.

Bengoa stood, walked over to the dusty record player, turned it on, and put the needle down on Beethoven's Pastoral.

"Do you know what this is?" he asked in a tone of voice that was new for him.

"It's Beethoven," Argenis replied. "Symphony no. 6."

"No." And he lowered the volume before sitting down in front of the checkers again. "It's the sound of greed."

The joyful notes from the opening of the Pastoral grated against the doctor's short tone. "This house you see here, Fidel gave it to me. Fidel himself. He gave it to me in one piece in 1962, just the way the *gusanos* had left it when they fled the revolution, when they ran away from justice, like the worms they were. I left this room just the way it was given to me. I've never taken the record from its place. It was the last thing those rats heard. It reminds me that people like you exist, people who believe they deserve it all."

Bengoa stood again and informed him: "José Alfredo hasn't sent anything for a month and a half. I've been taking care of everything – the apartment, the medicine, everything."

Argenis was suffocating, soaking in sweat. He wanted to die. Bengoa went over to the record player and took the needle off the Beethoven. Argenis followed him to the door in silence, and there he concluded: "You can stay in the apartment one more month, because I have great respect for Comrade Luna. But you'll have to find a way to pay for the medicine, because I can't keep taking it from the clinic for free."

Two vials for a pair of socks. One for a used T-shirt. Six for the pack of Fruit of the Loom underwear. He had already taken Bengoa the cans of tuna and beans, a pack of Santo Domingo coffee, a towel, and a bar of Protex soap, along with the Bic razor blades, a pair of jeans, and two Tommy Hilfiger polo shirts. He didn't want the belt because he was a lot bigger than Argenis and it didn't fit. One good day, he'd gotten three vials for a container of baby powder and four for the half-bottle of Old Spice aftershave.

Each day at noon, Argenis would stand in front of the suitcases and select the next currency to be exchanged. Susana cursed Bengoa and tried to convince him that quitting the Temgesic would be a lot more productive. She didn't know what withdrawal was, and Argenis had no intention of explaining it to her. She had stayed with him in spite of the fact that Bengoa was no longer paying her, and that every day took them further and further from the life they had been planning with those 500 dollars, a sum of money that was as imaginary as his studio and his career as an artist. They ate whatever she brought from her mother's house, because everything Argenis's mother had sent was now sitting in Bengoa's pantry. When he gave Susana the Case Logic full of CDs to exchange for money to call his father from the Hotel Nacional, she came back with canned ham, five pounds of rice, and a box of plums. The only thing they had left was the boom box.

You never know what you have until you lose it, Argenis thought. Lacking both money and Temgesic, his pockets were bursting with clichés. He took the boom box downstairs, planning to ask no fewer than twenty vials for it. They would let him endure another ten days, but after that, unless a miracle occurred, he'd have to get clean. He eyed the bronze bannister and calculated the force that would be needed to rip a piece of it off, like other desperate neighbors had already done.

He lit up a Popular to give himself something to do on the way. The city was looking particularly empty. The occasional slow-moving cars hardly made a sound, and from the enormous silence the squeaking of Chinese bicycles rose up like a witch's cackle. No smell of food, no perfume, no fruit-scented cleaning product wafted through any open door that afternoon. Only the bony faces of older women in housedresses, cooling off in a breeze that blew ferociously in their minds.

Argenis had taken longer than necessary to decide. In the absence of other options, the boom box – and the CD still inside, the greatest hits of the Allman Brothers – had become an extremely important source of well-being. Susana cried when she saw him unplug it and he promised that soon, after he had talked to his parents, they would have a much better stereo.

In the Parque de la Fraternidad, at the exit from Chinatown, Argenis saw an old man sitting on a bench, using a toothpick to fish around in one of his molars for some bothersome residue, a bit of meat or a grain of rice. The scene took him back to the recurrent memory of Argenis's grandmother Consuelo. She was cleaning the rice in a punch bowl, in the kitchen of the house where she'd worked her whole life. She took out the husks and the rotten grains and threw them away. Then she pulled out a rock with two fingers.

A rock had saved Zeus from being devoured by his father, a rock concealed in clothing, which Saturn ate thinking it was his son. His mother knew what José Alfredo was capable of and she had filled Argenis's suitcases with rocks for Saturn. Bengoa was the mouth his father had used to chew him up. If Argenis remembered the legend right, someday he would manage to defeat him. He'd get the Titan to vomit up everything he had swallowed, starting with the boom box.

It was the sort of toy car Santa Claus would bring you for Christmas when your parents couldn't afford a remote-controlled one. A little sports car with a hole in the back, through which you had to stick a plastic strip that made the wheels go round when you pulled it out with the movement you'd use to start a boat motor. Then you'd put the car on the floor and it would move forward, losing speed until it stopped completely. Argenis could see the details of that car as if he held it in his hand. Red, with a black circle around an orange flame on each side. Neither the doors, nor the hood, nor the trunk would open, and through the glassless windows you could see, right where the seats should be, the rudimentary mechanism that made the thing go. A cheap toy, made in China, the kind they sold in the wholesale shops along Mella Avenue.

When he saw himself stick the little plastic snake in the toy and pull it out again, an intense pain filled his intestines, throat, and nostrils, as if a giant version of the same strip had been poked in and out of all his orifices. It obscured everything, including the little car, in a long, hot stabbing which dissipated in bursts that grew further and further apart. He opened his eyes and saw the face of Che Guevara on the poster that had been hung on the closet door with four rusty thumbtacks. He concentrated on the star on

Che's black beret like on the light at the end of a tunnel. He counted the whistles of pain as they got further and further away, like a train behind the mountains. Then he felt relief and the thirst he would quench by drinking, if he had the strength to reach it, from an aluminum can full of water that smelled of burnt gasoline, like everything in Havana.

The cursive font on the poster read, "Words instruct, examples lead." He breathed deeply and noticed a slight smell of vomit on the pillowcase. Janet Jackson's "Nasty Boys" could clearly be heard through the wall. He could also hear the worn-out soles of his neighbor Vantroi's Reebok Classics squeaking on the tiles as he rehearsed Janet's choreography for one of his drag queen shows. Made useless by the withdrawal, Argenis had spent the last week in bed, but whenever he managed to find the strength he went out on the balcony for a little air. He had seen Vantroi leave the building a couple of times and he was never wearing the Adidas Argenis had given him.

Now that he had nothing left to trade for a vial of Temgesic, he saw those Adidas in a new light. Eyes closed and breathing deeply, the way he had learned to postpone the next wave of nausea and cramps, he speculated as to how many vials he could get for the sneakers. A disembodied hand opened in front of him with three, five, two, one vial. Again, he could smell the scent of newness the shoes had given off that afternoon when, like a junkie Mother Theresa, he gave those treasures away to a transvestite.

Would they look really used now? The question destabilized the slow breaths that kept his malaise at bay, filling his hands with sweat and something else. It was a little car. Santa Claus had brought him it at Christmas. He hadn't asked for it. The car was Chinese red and the flame adorning each side was poorly executed with stencil and spray paint on the plastic body. He knew what would happen next: he would put the band inside the toy's rear end and pull it out violently. He knew that the imaginary car would not move, and that it would disappear with the arrival of a pain that would lock him in a fetal position under his filthy sheet.

What was Bengoa's shoe size? Would he accept the Adidas in exchange for a box of vials?

Argenis had seen Bengoa's feet once, when the doctor was washing his brick-colored Russian car in front of his house. Like the rest of his anatomy, his feet were hairy and square, like wolf paws. The symmetry of his false teeth also reminded Argenis of an animal, although he didn't know which one.

Months ago, on the way to the airport in Santo Domingo, his dad had said to his mom, "Bengoa is a brother in arms," referring to their old revolutionary fervor. Sitting quietly in the back seat, Argenis had listened to them celebrating the brilliance of Chávez and the achievements of the Dominican volleyball team and its new Cuban coach. The divorce was ancient history and they now chitchatted like old friends, talking about Argenis in the third person. Bengoa and Susana had talked about him in the same way as he had twisted in pain in that broken bed. As if he didn't exist. "Did he drink any water?" "How many times did he go to the bathroom?" In his mind, Argenis offered Bengoa the T-shirt he was wearing, a Police T-shirt the doctor had once complimented him on and that now smelled of various secretions, in exchange for 1cc of Temgesic.

Bengoa came over almost every afternoon to see how he was doing. He'd take his pulse, check his blood pressure, make cruel jokes about diarrhea and nausea. "This will make you a man," he'd said, "a real, honest-to-God man." Then he'd ask Susana for coffee or a soda and both would leave the room. Argenis would follow the doctor's tenor voice through the apartment, his disorderly laugh, the way he dragged the chairs before sitting in them, until the apartment's front door would shut and Susana would again enter the room, to get him to drink a broth she'd made from the garlic and plantains Bengoa had so generously brought.

Unlike those invalids in books who lose all sense of time, Argenis knew perfectly well how many days it had been since his last fix. When he was free from the vision of the car, he counted the minutes on the plastic wall clock he had moved to his bedroom the day the vials ran out, knowing that after a certain number of days the withdrawal syndrome would end, but the minutes were long, being, as they were, full of pain and holograms on repeat.

Vantroi finished rehearsing and Argenis heard him rummaging through his dented drawers for lipstick and nylon stockings on the other side of the wall. That night Vantroi would be Janet Jackson at a makeshift club at a house in Vedado. Argenis would take advantage of Vantroi's absence and, filled with miraculous health, go up to the roof of the building, slip through the neighbor's balcony, and take back the sneakers, for which he meant to get a month's worth of vials from Bengoa.

Lacking energy, he ran through the operation in his mind. Barefoot and dressed in jean shorts and the tattered Police T-shirt, he would go up to the roof, burning his feet on bricks that were hot enough to fry an egg. He would slither to the edge of the eaves overhanging his neighbor's balcony and lean his head and torso over, holding on with both hands, hanging there for a second like a bat on the darkening Havana horizon. He would enter the transvestite's house, listening to his own pulse hammering against the walls of reinforced concrete. When he got to the bedroom he would be surprised by the cleanliness with which Vantroi countered the deterioration of the furniture. He would open the wardrobe and find women's high-heeled shoes and men's moccasins. He would not find the Adidas, now that they were part of the Janet Jackson costume, but rather Vantroi's stinking Reebok Classics.

They were the same model of Reebok Classics Argenis had asked Santa for when he was eight. Half of the boys in his class at the Nuevo Amanecer school already had them, while he was still wearing "kukiká" sneakers, which is what his classmates called cheap, fake, or Chinese brands. His parents were still together back then, and when his mother had seen the yellow report card with his improved grades that December of 1985, she had said to Argenis, while winking at his father, that Santa would certainly be bringing him the sneakers he wanted so badly.

That Saturday José Alfredo had taken him along to sell the *Vanguard of the People*, the newspaper of the Dominican Liberation Party, an organization to which he dedicated all his spare time and whose ascent he would preach through-out the barrios of Santo Domingo in his cream-colored *guay-abera* and the dated bell-bottom pants which embarrassed Argenis whenever he came to pick him up from school. In some of the houses they were welcomed with coffee and cookies, dulce de leche, or buttery caramels with which Argenis would fill his pockets. But on that day, when they reached the driveway of Tony Catrain, his dad's best friend, the man, dressed in a modern sports suit, greeted them without a glance and carelessly tossed the ten newspapers José Alfredo had brought him into the back seat of his SUV.

José Alfredo didn't open his mouth in the *concho* the whole way to Ciudad Nueva, or as they walked along El Conde while black, white, and red Reeboks smiled through the shop windows of Los Muchachos and Calzados Lama. He took little Argenis to a *colmado,* a corner store where four men were smacking their dominoes down onto a square table, with sardine cans and Brugal bottles lined up on shelves behind them like sailors in the February 27 parade. They sat on a bench and his father ordered a small bottle of Ron Macorix and a Pepsi. He opened the rum and gave the Pepsi to Argenis. They toasted and drank the contents of both bottles too fast. When his father set the empty rum bottle on the counter, he was crying. "Son," he said, squeezing the boy's shoulder, "today is a special day. I have to tell you something because I can't bear you being lied to. Do you know who Santa Claus is?" Argenis said he did. "It's me," said José Alfredo, slapping his chest with a slight tremor on his lips. "I use my money to buy the stuff you ask for. The Yankees invented Santa Claus," he said, looking out on the street with its high, sunny sidewalks. "They invented him to make people buy junk." Argenis knew his father didn't have a job so he imagined his mom in the red suit and beard coming down a chimney. He felt an enormous desire to protect the man whose nose was running the way his own did in the schoolyard when they teased him about his cheap sneakers.

"The world is changing and your dad is getting left behind," his father said and ordered a roll with white cheese, which he tore in two. "My friends go around in nice clothes, and here I am in these old rags." His father looked at him steadily, with bloodshot eyes and a little bit of cheese on his mustache. "Do you see that over there?" he asked, pointing to a sign that said TAILOR. "There, they could make an elegant suit your dad could use to get ahead."

Without letting go of his empty Pepsi, Argenis asked, "And why don't they, Papi?" "Because Papi has no money,"

José Alfredo responded, stroking his son's head in short, repetitive motions, like Aladdin with his famous lamp.

They left the *colmado* and José Alfredo took his hand to cross the street. Now, in the tailor's doorway, looking at the ground and grimacing, he said, "Your mom gave me money to get your sneakers. What brand was it you wanted? I forget." With a sense of duty that hardly fit in his body, Argenis purged himself of the need of a pair of brand-name shoes, of his fear of the jokes his friends would continue to make as they pointed at his sneakers, and pulled his trembling father into the tailor's.

They entered a narrow space at the rear of which a table was stacked to the ceiling with fabric. The memory of the hot, clean smell of that place invaded his room in Havana. It was the steam an iron brings out of the starched cloth of a shirt. Next to the table a doorway led to a workshop. There, two dark-skinned young men, their gazes fixed on sewing machines, were finishing something that looked like a costume. One was decorating the edge of a pair of pants with ribbon, the other was completing a fuchsia vest. Argenis thought of the outfits of the bands of Tony Seval or Aramis Camilo. A short man in gray cashmere pants and a pale-gray shirt bustled about with his back to them, a measuring tape around his neck, an iron in his hand, and a cigarette in his mouth. When he turned around to greet them, smiling, Argenis could make out the glimmer of a gold tooth in place of one of his canines under the very black, triangular mustache.

His father's suit was already finished. When José Alfredo saw it he let go of Argenis's hand to try it on, and there, in front of everyone, shed his clothes as fast as someone with only twenty minutes to cheat on their wife. It was a dark-blue two-piece suit. Once it was on, his dad made a James

Bond face in the mirror on the wall, not seeing the boy who watched him from a palm-wicker chair in the corner of the reflection.

After recovering the memory of this event Argenis hated Vantroi's old shoes even more, but he didn't have the energy to maintain his hatred of them for even a minute, much less to get to the actual wardrobe. He was still in the bedroom of an apartment painted in watered-down pink. On the wall was another poster, one on which Castro stood gesticulating on a podium, over the phrase "Patria o Muerte, venceremos!" Eighties sneakers had aged better than these slogans, thought Argenis, hearing the soles of Vantroi's marking the beat of a song. It seemed that Vantroi was still rehearsing, producing that rhythmic scuffing. The sound became more defined and Argenis could now hear it throughout his apartment. But Susana would never allow Vantroi to practice in the living room. He stretched his leg out, full of tracks where he'd occasionally injected himself to give his arm a rest, and he stuck his big toe into the crack to open the door. At the end of the hall in the living room, Bengoa was fucking Susana on the rattan sofa. He was sticking his sausage-colored penis in from behind, holding her by the waist, both of them facing Argenis's room and lying on their sides on cushions patterned with tropical flowers. The doctor's khaki-colored balls were hanging to one side and, still wearing his glasses, he was sticking out a long, red tongue which he used to touch the little round pink one Susana offered him.

Motherfuckers, Argenis yelled with a strength he didn't have. When she realized that she'd been caught, Susana struggled to free herself, but the doctor held her firm and increased the speed of his hip thrusts until he pulled out his already-shrinking penis and came, his cum thick as a strand of fresh pasta. Argenis tried to get up out of bed as Susana fought with Bengoa, but like the little stars that go around Donald Duck's head when they whack him, the Reebok Classics, Bengoa's feet, and his father's tailor's gold tooth were whirling around his brain. His rage filled him with a strange vigor. He went out to the living room, dizzy but decisive. Bengoa was buttoning his pants with a little smile as vulgar as his hairy chest and Susana was crying in the kitchen, her clothes on all wrong. Argenis seized Dr. Bengoa's neck, but Bengoa was bigger and he wasn't sick. He extricated himself from the improvised noose with one hand, and foiled Susana's attempt to help Argenis by throwing them both to the ground. He punched his patient's ear, grabbed him by the T-shirt, opened the front door, and threw him out.

With the sun hidden, the stairway was in shadow. A modest erection foretold the end of the abstinence syndrome. As Argenis lay there on his side on the freezing cold floor, his ears buzzing, he remembered the tailor with his measuring tape, coming over to him with an anise candy in his hand to say, "One day, when you're big, I'll make you a suit." He touched the modest erection under his pants, put his hand inside and grabbed the little car. It was the car Santa had brought him that one Christmas, the little red "Made in China" car that his father, new plastic-wrapped suit over his shoulder, had made him choose from a display case full of old, dusty wholesale toys on Mella Avenue.

Instead of a nose he had a trunk. A disgusting, bleeding trunk. That's why it smelled like blood. Or vomit. A Pepto-Bismol-colored glue with which they'd stuck him to the floor. They had fused his eyelashes to the bronze of the art nouveau railing. When the next thief showed up to rip off a piece with a hacksaw, he was going to get a surprise. A man had been fused to the stairway railing. That, or the line for rice came this far. Old sidecars without motorcycles came this far. Pregnant guerrilla fighters, with their throats slit.

Something like the torment of a crown of thorns pressed into his temples. This was no Bible, this was pre-revolutionary architecture. Dr. Bengoa read his thoughts; he was his mother's gynaecologist. A glimmer of actual light made him notice the makeup of the images: they were made of air, like music. They shook him about. He had fallen asleep in front of the TV watching *Rocky III* and his dad had carried him to bed. His dad wearing lipstick. Vantroi wasn't his dad. Vantroi was Vantroi was Vantroi was Vantroi and he was Argenis, being funneled to wakefulness, to the unfamiliar bedroom where he had awoken, naked between white sheets.

He felt relief, no nausea, no pain, and sat up on a bed with a backboard of laurel-shaped metal leaves. The world had stopped spinning. He looked at his hand, his arm full of old track marks, swollen like ant bites, staring at the incredible length of his fingernails. The memory of what had happened during the days when sickness had him bound and gagged came to him from far away, as if through an IV. Someone had set the cleaned and folded Police T-shirt and jean shorts on a green plastic chair. At the foot of the chair sat the Adidas sneakers, inviting him to put them on. He opened the door, covering himself with the sheet, and confirmed he was at Vantroi's place when he saw the TV and the tower of VHS tapes. The apartment was empty. He went into the bathroom. Photos cut from black-and-white magazines completely covered the walls. As he peed, Mickey Mouse, Fred Astaire, Sônia Braga, Boy George, Marcello Mastroianni, and of course Janet Jackson, fixed their famous eyes on him. He got into the shower. The morning sun had warmed the water in the tank. He stood under the stream of water with his eyes open, as if to clean them from the inside. Not even if he yanked his eyes from his head could he ever forget Bengoa's penis entering Susana.

The soap bar was almost used up and it was full of kinky hair. He pulled the hairs out with his nails, cursing Bengoa and marveling again at how his nails had grown, at this raucous biological drive, immune to human disappointment. Nothing stops nails, he thought, scrubbing himself violently. He washed his armpits, his ass, his balls, rinsed his mouth, turned off the shower and dried himself with a wine-colored rag that had once been a towel. He remembered the blue towel he had shared with Susana during their time together. She would bathe in the morning so that it would be dry when it was his turn in the afternoon. He tried to remember a Lezama Lima poem about Havana's corrosive power as he dried off. Returning to the bedroom he put on his T-shirt and shorts, but not the shoes, and went out on the balcony.

From the eaves, from which he had imagined descending to steal the Adidas no time at all ago, Vantroi had hung a mobile, a little homemade Calder of wire and circular pieces of plastic milk jugs. It made him want to paint that little solar system onto the indigo band of the Atlantic in the background, onto the amalgam of crumbling cement roof-tops, the most frequently painted ruins of all the Antilles, worn away daily by a ridiculous proliferation of directors of mediocre music documentaries.

If he thought about the city rather than himself he could decipher the outlines of his new solitude, forcefully detached from his Temgesic dependence, from Bengoa, from romantic love, from his father. He did not feel any self-pity; he was floating in space under little plastic planets with the names of gods. There was already a star named Vantroi in his personal galaxy – not the Vietnamese communist, but the neighbor who had sheltered him. A stray breeze brought to his ears the new jack swing of Janet Jackson's "Rhythm Nation", which was playing out on the rooftop terrace. Vantroi had moved his rehearsal upstairs so as not to bother him.

He climbed the stairs, following the rhythmic shouts of the beginning of the song. Vantroi was dancing on the little pink stage, blasting the music on an old, battery-powered tape recorder. Argenis ducked behind the water tank like an urban guerrilla and from there spied on his neighbor. He remembered the choreographies he'd put together with Charlie, Tony Catrain's son, in the schoolyard. It was 1990 and house music was bursting out from all speakers. It was all steps they'd seen on MTV videos, just before discovering the Doors and Led Zeppelin. Vantroi threw sparks of sweat into the air as he executed the rigid, symmetric movements from the video. He was wearing boots that could only have been a present from his cousin Juani in Chicago, together with the hot pants he'd had on the first time Argenis had seen him peering into the water tank. He wore no shirt, as was his custom, and the contracted muscles of his torso reflected light from the sky like a living Rodin.

Resonant metallic beats like clashing swords punched Argenis in the stomach, and he felt the same intense desire to dance that at thirteen had moved all his friends whenever they heard Technotronic. It was a powerful sensation, the same one that makes fingernails want to grow, he thought, marking the rhythm with his bare feet. In his mind he ran through a short sequence of what Vantroi was breaking into four-counts. He saw himself as part of the dark underground army in the video: a fin-de-siècle Black Panther dressed in leather with stainless-steel insignia, fighting a musical battle against psychological complexes and bad memories. Not even Bengoa's penis could rob him of the desire to move to the beat of that song.

Vantroi saw him and burst out laughing. "Boy, you've got good rhythm," he said, weaving his words together with his deep and contagious laugh. He had a space between his two front teeth, like Madonna, and a little pink button nose well suited to transvestism. He came down from the stage with the tape recorder in his hand and passed it to Argenis to hold as he drank water from a metal jug in the shadow of the tank.

"You're looking better. How do you feel?" he asked. "Much better," said Argenis. "Thanks for –" Vantroi didn't let him finish. "Thanks for nothing, boy. What was I going to do – leave you there shitting yourself in the stairway?" They went down to Vantroi's place and Argenis couldn't help listening for Susana's voice in the apartment that had formerly been his. "She came to see you before she left, but you were asleep," Vantroi said as he opened the door, showing him the empty red suitcase Susana had left in a corner of the living room. "Do you have anyone here in Cuba?" he asked from the kitchen as he put coffee grounds into the pot.

"No, no one. Just my doctor." When he said "doctor" Argenis made air quotes. His host closed the coffee pot and, lighting the stove, said, "Boy, that guy's a creep. We'll have to find you something – what can you do?"

He could recognize cocaine that had been cut with acetone. Come up with excuses. Sponge off others. Prepare a syringe full of heroin. Shoot up. He could cook rice, rice that was hard and flavorless. He looked at his hands, huge and bony, with yellowed palms, much lighter than the rest of his body. They itched. "Do you have a pencil and paper?" he asked Vantroi. His host opened a kitchen cabinet and pulled out a stub of a Berol Mirado and a piece of manila paper on which someone had written a list of materials that included Wiki-Wiki black dye and baseball caps.

"Stand over there," he told Vantroi, pointing toward the balcony, so that the tender light of a sky just starting to cloud over would hit his profile. He flipped the page over to use the blank side and his fingers closed around the inch of pencil like the petals of a cayenne flower when night falls. Then he made the graphite dance over the paper almost effortlessly until he had turned his savior's flesh into a beautiful convergence of dark lines.

Vantroi's mother was a huge woman with fists of steel who had exhorted her son to "Be a fag, but not a pussy." When he came home from school with his first bruise, she hit him with a belt right on the mark and threatened to kill him if he let them hit him again. From then on, he defended himself from the world tooth and nail, sure that if he didn't the woman would keep her promise. Brígida had died when she was hit by a car during the Special Period, as she was bringing three pounds of ground beef home in her skirt. On the wall of Vantroi's apartment hung a youthful photo of her dressed in a military uniform in 1962, part of a group who was laughing at a shirtless Che's jokes, as he carried out voluntary labor with a shovel in his hand. Vantroi had his mother's smile, and the muscles and honey-colored eyes of his father, a musician from Matanzas who had died before Vantroi turned four.

That body Vantroi had inherited was posing on the rooftop stage in a G-string, so that Argenis could fill bits of cardboard with drawings of it. His hand was practiced, despite it having been a long time since he'd last worked, and the lines came out sure and inspired, except when he asked himself what Susana would think of the sketches. Then a certain melancholy would infiltrate his steady hand, a melancholy that populated his curves with tiny vibrations.

The morning sun gushed over his model, who changed position every ten minutes, laughing and commenting on all the failures Argenis recounted for him, the sequence of clusterfucks that, deserved or not, had followed him ever since he had left the Altos de Chavón art school.

Having accumulated a number of sketches, Argenis asked Vantroi to come down from the stage and sit by him. Over the top of those bodies, he drew various outfits and accessories, triangular forms that emulated the heads of Wifredo Lam creatures, the post-apocalyptic armor of *Mad Max*, and the magical signatures of the Palo Mayombe religion. He was aiming for a heavy metal/rumba aesthetic, as he ate some mashed potatoes Vantroi had brought up in a saucepan. A George Michael cassette that a pen pal had sent to Vantroi from Prague in the eighties played in the background. Next to the TV and the VHS tapes in the living room Vantroi had two boxes full of letters he'd received from friends all over the world, with whom he shared his literary and musical interests. Sometimes they sent gifts: colored pencils, stickers, photos of artists torn from magazines. Many of them arrived already open. "They read them before they give them to you, as if you're going to plan a coup by correspondence," Vantroi told him. "Like it's the fifth century or something."

Argenis tried to imagine the dimensions of that kind of claustrophobia, but he couldn't. His friend had been asking permission to leave the country since he was twenty-one. Now he was thirty-seven. He surprised himself by making plans to get Vantroi out of Cuba, but all of them involved his father, José Alfredo, who still spoke of the Cuban Revolution as if it were a living thing, a good thing, clinging to the worn-out luster of a few social achievements on top of which repression in all its forms had been piled. How easy it was to hang the framed photo of the *comandante* in the living room of an apartment in Naco, its refrigerator full of imported cheeses, fresh vegetables, and ten pounds of *churrasco* meat his father would consume rare with a bottle of Marqués de Murrieta several times a week, ever since the PLD's first win in 1996, when he'd taken a couple of classes in etiquette and manners. He thought of his Aunt Niurka, his father's sister, who had never boasted any militancy whatsoever, but who gave everything she had to others on a daily basis. After graduating in Madrid with a degree in psychiatry, she had dedicated herself to helping abused low-income women. He'd have to get the money together to call her and ask for a plane ticket or some cash.

As he descended the stairs back to Vantroi's apartment, hands full of sketches, he felt a pleasurable sensation of calm. With those bits of cardboard he could pay Vantroi back for the roof over his head and the food he'd been offered. For the first time in his life, he could live off his art. The overly salty potatoes the Cuban Vantroi shared with him were bombshells of friendship, of a nameless brotherhood constructed around creativity and beauty.

He arranged the drawings on the floor in the light coming off the balcony and imagined them as monumental paintings, murals on the sides of Santo Domingo's modern buildings. He felt the breeze that would buffet him up there on the tall scaffold, the tension in his hands as he moved a roller that would spread the paint along the hair on a huge, black head.

Vantroi walked on ahead, wearing his tattered pre-washed jeans, turquoise high heels – executive-secretary-style – a sleeveless silk blouse the color of a *zapote* fruit, and, over his head and shoulders, a threadbare yellow pashmina. Argenis followed behind over the thirty or so blocks, dragging one of the red suitcases with which he'd arrived in Cuba, currently full of all the costumes and scenery needed for Vantroi's next show. He regretted having been so creative, now that the weight of all the materials they'd gathered on errands all over Havana was making his balls swell. The temperature suddenly dropped and Vantroi arranged the pashmina to protect himself from the wind with a gesture borrowed from Claudia Cardinale, if Claudia Cardinale were one half of a duo of artistic beggars. As they passed by the parish church of the Sacred Heart the scene was complete: it was the living image of the Five of Pentacles in the Rider-Waite tarot deck. On the card, a pair of mendicants pass by a church's stained-glass window: a woman walks ahead, cloaked in a rag, and a crippled man follows her on crutches. It was the card of poverty, of bankruptcy caused by emotional instability. In 2001, Argenis had worked as a psychic on a telephone line that offered personalized readings all over the United States, and he knew the cards by heart. No one there possessed any special powers, but they made them learn the meanings of the oracles, how to improvise and do free association. He didn't need his cards dealt to know that he had become the Minor Arcana of poverty.

As they left the temple behind, one of the wheels of the suitcase fell off and Argenis bent down to fix it, without success. He'd have to carry the bag the rest of the way. In silence he begged, God, give me a break, and sped up, with the heavy suitcase in his arms as if this demonstration of vigor and determination were a substitute for faith. The effort brought an avalanche of sadness down upon him and he dropped the bag to sit on the curb and cry. Vantroi offered him the pashmina to blow his nose on. He couldn't get the image of Susana out of his head, inconsolable and half-naked in the kitchen the day he'd caught her with Bengoa. He looked at the hand that had been dragging the suitcase, the fluid-filled blister on the thumb. As he poked it with a finger to make the bubble burst, the church bells tolled six o'clock. The peals were so weak and distant that Argenis wondered if the ringing was real or if he was imagining it. He had been confusing certain sounds ever since his brother Ernesto had convinced him to put a piece of Lego in his ear when he was three. The memory of the little blood-stained block in the doctor's tweezers still made his eardrum hurt.

When would he be able to go back to Santo Domingo? What would he go back to? After years of conscientiously descending the rungs of the food chain, he'd finally reached the bottom. He saw himself pushing a shopping cart full of trash, beer cans, and dirty stuffed animals along Lincoln Avenue, wearing shoes made of trash bags and fly larvae in his beard. The image of his mother in a housedress came uninvited and put a wrinkle in his pessimism. Etelvina was beating him with a broom, shouting, "You turd, you piece of shit," hitting him with the broom handle in the parking lot of the building where he'd grown up, in front of all the neighbors. The idea made him laugh. He stood up and caressed the handle of the red suitcase. It was all he had left. That, Vantroi's friendship, and the promise they'd made to share the money they'd earn from their *Rhythm Nation* show in Coribantes, the event space into which Iñaki, a young Spanish architect, turned his Vedado mansion every weekend.

Iñaki's house reminded him of the Gazcue neighborhood of his childhood. It was practically identical to the villa that had housed his elementary school, a school for children of leftists and feminists, an experimental school where his mom worked so that she would only need to pay half-tuition for him and his brother Ernesto. Both the Vedado house and the one in Santo Domingo's Gazcue had been built in the thirties. They belonged to the well-to-do that had migrated north in the second half of the twentieth century – those from Havana to Miami, and those from Santo Domingo to the outskirts of the city; the former fleeing Castro and the latter fleeing a proletariat that had made enough money in New York to buy and mutilate the old edifices, turning them into boarding houses, corner stores, beauty salons, and internet cafés.

Like all buildings in Cuba, Coribantes had to contend with a lack of materials for repairs. Time had traced an intricate series of cracks all over the salmon-colored walls. The porch, spanned end to end by an arch, sprouted a rounded marble staircase along whose edges bannisters descended like rivulets of condensed milk and spilled over the cement cookie at the stairway's base. Asymmetrical chunks missing from the marble of the staircase sullied the house's old-man smile. The ferns and *lenguas de vaca* in the front yard were the only sign of life in the whole ensemble.

The door was open and from it emerged two anorexic young queens carrying a papier-mâché Venus de Milo. Inside, the vestiges of a chic past – furniture, lamps, rugs, and designer ashtrays – looked much newer than the filthy exterior walls. The long mahogany bar bore witness to the parties held there before the guys with beards forbade fun. From the bar hung a sign with the word CORIBANTES in gold sequins on silver fabric. A spiral staircase led up to the second-floor bedrooms, and on the mezzanine below a stage with a dressing room occupied what must once have been a music room. They dragged the suitcase up onto the stage and behind the curtains to the dressing room, but when they tried to open its zipper, the fabric ripped from one end to the other. A gold chain, a cow's horn, a femur, and a black *rumbero* sleeve its owner had claimed once belonged to Kike Mendive spilled through the wound. Vantroi had pulled the chain off a neighbor's door, received the cow horn as a gift from a *santera* who had used its shavings in certain particularly aggressive spiritual cleansings, traded a clandestine butcher a tiny perfume sample for the pig's femur, and acquired Kike's shirt sleeve from an ex-lover who had been a grandson of the illustrious *rumbero*.

Armed with a staple gun, Argenis occupied himself with draping the columns and uppermost beam on the stage with black fabric. It was really discarded hospital sheets they'd dyed with Wiki-Wiki, though the blood and shit stains eluded all efforts at cleaning; the ink had seeped into the stained parts less forcefully, creating a streaked appearance. From the top of each column he used wire to hang human skulls provided by a student at the University of Medical Sciences. Strips of wine-colored cloth, part of the interior upholstery of his suitcases, emerged like vomit from the mouths of the skulls. From the central beam he hung bits of bone, eyeless doll heads, and spiny bougain-villea stems he'd painted red, like mobiles of horror. The backdrop, made from another recycled and dyed sheet, was covered in splatters of red paint, abstract scribbles, and spiky symbols.

When the stage was ready, they went out onto the patio to eat a few boxes of rice and pork Iñaki had brought for them. They sat next to a drained swimming pool in the shade of an enormous mango tree whose rotten fruits were being pecked by a black chicken at the bottom of the pool. The pork was cold and possibly spoiled, but Vantroi swallowed it almost without chewing. In Santo Domingo Argenis would never have put such a thing in his mouth, but he was hungry and so he held his breath. For the first time he felt the urge to shoot up, and he calculated how many Temgesic vials he would be able to get in exchange for one of the Johnny Walker bottles he'd seen behind the bar. He lay down on the floor on his back and relaxed, detaching himself from the desire to use, understanding the means by which it had arisen, until little by little he rid himself of his anxiety. With eyes closed, he went over the costume he'd designed for his friend: the military pants dyed black, his cousin Juani's black boots, the chain belt. The red scraps of curtain that would cross the dark face makeup and torso like dried blood, the lipstick outlining the soft, womanly mouth that would hide teeth covered in aluminum foil, the black *rumbero*-sleeved shirt, and a beret like Che's from whose center sprouted not a star but a cow's horn, like Dagoth's magic horn in *Conan the Destroyer*. He had filled the beret with stuffing so it wouldn't lose its shape, so it would stay fixed in place during the choreography and could thus crown the monstrous revolutionary cadaver Vantroi would become.

Whenever he actually made the effort, something of the images called up through his art would transfer into reality. During the show, the smell of the dead pig and the rotten mangos on the patio stuck in his nose. His creation pounded the stage with nineties steps to the beat of "Rhythm Nation." The creature was far from anything you'd see in a typical drag show, but the audience of foreigners, Cuban artists, and queers of all types clapped to the beat of the song. In spite of the enthusiasm, the atmosphere was charged. What forces were that dark death's mask drawing to it? A man's hand broke through the wall of smoke surrounding the stage to approach the dancer with a few dollars, putting the bills in the horror of a mouth. The devil bit the money violently, as if it wanted to pull off the fingers of his fan, whom Argenis recognized when one of the spotlights illuminated his face. It was Bebo Conde, a Dominican and a former classmate at Altos de Chavón, where Bebo had studied graphic design and Argenis fine art. Back then Bebo hadn't yet come out of the closet, and he'd fucked all the women Argenis dreamed of having. Years later, after the divorce, his expulsion from school, the loss of his scholarship, the whole debacle, it was Bebo who had gotten him to try heroin for the first time, one morning after they left a rave at Playa Caribe, as they watched the sun rise while lying on the hood of an old Honda CRX. The unrepeatable intensity of that first pleasure was the yardstick against which he measured everything in life. His addiction was really an eternal pursuit of that momentary abolition of guilt, need, responsibility, and introspection.

Bebo Conde's apartment was dark, except for the lighting kit Bebo had taken without permission from the film school at San Antonio de los Baños, where he'd come to study. The spotlights illuminated the back of the living room, where he had hung a green cloth that smoothed all the angles of the wall and the floor. In front of the improvised green screen, an Asian girl in a bikini and a Vietcong rice farmer's hat danced provocatively, without music. Samanta wore a straight-haired blonde wig and fake eyelashes in the same color, which opened like the teeth of a carnivorous plant around her eyes. Bebo was directing her from behind a fat German who manned the camera and Argenis wondered what the girl's little yellow tits would taste like. He walked to the kitchen, without greeting a couple of students involved in various production details, opened the refrigerator just as he would have in Bebo's Santo Domingo home, and took out a bottle of Perrier. He had to do some acrobatics to avoid tripping over the boxes full of cans of beans, toilet paper, and Barilla toothpaste Bebo brought every other month from Santo Domingo, which he used to pay his classmates for their work on the improvised set.

"Did you bring the shit?" Bebo asked, pulling him by the sleeve to show him a laptop playing animations he'd add behind Samanta in postproduction, a series of concentric circles in different colors that Argenis, nodding, judged as better suited to a screen saver than a music video. Bebo called time on the shoot and the team dispersed onto a little open terrace, led by Samanta, who'd covered herself with a very fluffy wine-colored terrycloth robe. Bebo might be a fag, but he was surely doing it with *la china*, Argenis thought. They walked to Bebo's bedroom and locked the door. Argenis pulled a strip of Temgesic vials from his pocket as Bebo tore open the packaging of the disposable syringe with his teeth. Lying on his side on the bed, he offered it to Argenis, who stuck it into the ampoule, then felt for Bebo's vein under his athletic socks. They touched each other with the familiarity of addiction, a familiarity Argenis shared with no other man. Bebo had recently cleaned himself up in a private clinic in Santo Domingo, but both of them would have found it suspect or offensive if the other hadn't asked if in Cuba there was any "H", which is what they'd called heroin whenever they shot up listening to Lou Reed in Bebo's parents' music room.

To get Bengoa to open the door, he'd had to show the fifty-dollar bill Bebo had given him for the errand through the window. Bengoa sold him thirty-five dollars' worth of Temgesic, Argenis had given him an extra five as an incentive, and he'd kept the remaining ten. That five-dollar tip he'd given the doctor had made Argenis feel quite comfortable, so much so that he asked, in a voice too nasal to be natural, if Bengoa was still nailing Susana. "You're such an idiot," Bengoa said, counting out the vials. "She only did it for you, so that I'd bring you food and medicine." The revelation had hit him like a ton of bricks. He was still trying to get it out of his body when Bebo, ready as ever, closed his eyes so that Argenis could inject him in the orange afternoon light by which they always did these things.

Under the effects of the synthetic morphine, Bebo was even more beautiful. His muscles, toned by sports like the tennis and swimming he'd practiced in his parents' backyard, were covered in a soft, smooth, golden fuzz. Whenever they were open, the fleshy mouth and gypsy eyes stood out from his face. Bebo also had a telephone, one of those devices that in Santo Domingo you'd only find in the Little Haiti flea market behind the Mercado Modelo, and from which no international calls could be made.

He was tempted to take a vial himself. A burst of pleasure traveled down his spine just thinking about it. He glanced at the ones that were still lying on top of a Cuban edition of Stanislavski's *An Actor Prepares* on the nightstand. Injecting Bebo without injecting himself was the proof that he was healthy, that this time he was clean for real. He had displaced the desire and that desire had been transferred to his friend's body so that Argenis could keep feeding it there, like a father responsible for his ex-wife and children. He had a thousand reasons to start shooting up again but an even more powerful one for not doing it: his Aunt Niurka, who was expecting his call. His Aunt Niurka, who had promised to help him. The memory of his Aunt Niurka playing "I Spy" with him on the way to Boca Chica in the minivan she'd rent whenever she visited the DR with her Spanish friends who smoked like chimneys.

I spy with my little eye. What do you spy? A thing. What color is it? Gold. What size? Small. What's it made out of? Metal. Iron? No, gold. Your rings? Your earrings? And so on, for half an hour.

A clue? It's in the hand of an angel. Argenis searched for an answer in the giant clouds in the sky on both sides of the highway. Later, tired, his gaze fell unaided on the little holy card of Archangel San Miguel that hung from the rear-view mirror. In his right hand the sword, raised over a demon ablaze under the boot of the celestial soldier. In his left, the golden scale of divine justice.

To call his aunt he'd have to walk to the Hotel Nacional and pay an arm and a leg for just a few minutes. Bebo's wallet and passport were on the nightstand. Without asking, Argenis picked up the turquoise leather wallet and looked inside. A wad of dollars in various denominations stopped it from closing completely. Using two fingers like tweezers, he pulled out eighty dollars and returned the wallet to its place, thinking that the privileges his friend enjoyed could serve as proof of reincarnation just as effectively as those children with flies in their eyes on the UNICEF ads. He brought the new bills to his nose. They were so new that he could have cut a slice of ripe papaya with their edges. Bebo must have been a saint in his previous life and he himself must have been Trujillo, at the very least. Blessed by abundance, money was just an abstraction to Bebo, a concept lacking in that curly head his barber always cut in the style of a Roman emperor.

Bebo asked for a blanket. At this point, all of his plans for the day were canceled, except for reading the poem "7:00 on the Nose" by Virgilio Piñera, which he recited like a rosary every night at the time of the title. Argenis handed him a pink blanket that was hanging on the back of a chair and Bebo wrapped himself in it from head to toe. Under the blanket Argenis found a cream-colored sport jacket, hung there so it wouldn't lose its shape, a jacket Bebo wore with Bermuda shorts and white T-shirts, and which, like everything he wore, fit as if he had been sewn into it. The label, embroidered in wine-colored thread on the garment's neck, attracted his attention. He picked it up and read the name of the tailor: Orestes Loudón. The name sounded familiar. "You'll have to wake up a little more," Bebo recited from inside the blanket, deciphering Piñera with a tiny flashlight. Argenis put the jacket on, looking at himself in the mirror Bebo had set across from the bed to enjoy the reflection of his lovers. Argenis's Police T-shirt gave an edgy touch to the blazer, but not the cut-off jeans. He peeled off his shorts and looked for something in the closet to wear, deciding on some brown cotton pants. "Remember it in the midst of your hell," Bebo whispered from inside the blanket as Argenis put them on. "It is your compass to the final north."

Admiring his new look, Argenis remembered his father, that morning in front of the tailor's mirror, trying on a custom-made suit he would pay for with his son's Christmas money. The smell of cigarettes and new fabric came to him, together with the name of the little man who was winking at him while his dad counted the bills out onto the sewing table. That same Loudón was the only witness to the debt his father had incurred with him that day, the memory of which Argenis had recovered during his illness, like a crumpled receipt in the bottom of a pocket. It was a memory much more valuable now than a suit. It was a debt that had accumulated interest, and Argenis was ready to collect on it.

He left the room and found the house as empty as the box of toilet paper that had been violently ripped open; Bebo's buddies had claimed their daily loot: the silky Charmin. Before Bebo had saved him from giving his ass to a Spaniard, he had already been scratching himself for months with Cuban toilet paper, a thin, rough paper that didn't protect your fingers from the shit at all.

He went down in an elevator lined with mirrors in which his head, a squarish but attractive head, was infinitely reflected. He felt a certain amount of pleasure and security allotted by Bebo's clothing, as if the costume he wore might throw his complexes off track. He pictured himself in a custom-made suit at the opening of his first solo exhibition. He pictured himself selling all his pieces, and some newspaper dedicating the front page of its culture supplement to him.

When he got to the Hotel Nacional, a security guard poked his chest with a sharp finger. "No nationals allowed here, buddy." Buddy, my ass, thought Argenis, as he took out his Dominican passport, a passport that would have brought him only trouble in half the world, but which here, thanks to the stupidities of the revolution, was as good as a Swiss one.

"Pardon me, sir." Apologizing, the guard pointed the way to the upholstered phone booths full of foreign voices from which he had called his Aunt Niurka for the first time a week ago on Bebo's dime. When his aunt picked up he could hear the sound of the Friday-evening traffic jam in front of her building in Santo Domingo on the other end of the line. She had returned from Europe not long ago and was renting an apartment on Bolívar Avenue, in the same Gazcue neighborhood Argenis was once again comparing with the dying Vedado.

Argenis missed those sounds: the swearing drivers, the frenetic tackiness, the trash besieged by thousands of flies on the curbs, the cell phone chargers, the plantains and loofahs, the swollen hands of Haitian beggars. He missed its filth. From time to time in the midst of the crowds you could feel something beautiful. A light that shone on everything, a color and a light that gave the commotion a secret meaning. Like a double-entendre song, only this time the song was vulgar and its hidden meaning sublime.

"So what does the artist have to say?" Niurka asked in a happy voice. "Whatever's left of him, you mean," Argenis responded. "Surprise! I bought you the ticket!" his aunt shouted. "Praise be," he said. "Did you go to Cuba to be born again?" she asked over the raucous honking of *conchos* and minivans. "The revolution works miracles, and so does Papi, the son of a bitch," Argenis said, chuckling a bit. Niurka knew the call was expensive, so to move things along she told him, "I have the confirmation number – do you have something to write with?"

Argenis stuck his head up over the cubicle and made the universal sign for writing, joining his thumb and index finger to draw a letter in the air. A German in Coke-bottle glasses passed him a black Sharpie and with it Argenis wrote the airline ticket confirmation number on his forearm. After hanging up, he left the hotel quickly so he wouldn't have to return the marker. Painted in darkness, Havana recovered something of its former glory, like an old whore when the lights are off. He would use these last hours to walk through it like a tourist. He'd admire the baroque architecture, the centuries-old *ceiba* trees, the wide European sidewalks, without any trick questions about anyone's lack of anything, nor about the imminent collapse of infinite ruins deposited like leftovers on a Titan's plate.

They were screams that pushed outward, bulging into the present like blood into a welt. He too had screamed like that before. In 2001, during an artistic residency on the coast, he had started to have visions of mutilated cows and headless buccaneers. His own screams had woken him in the night. He'd been kicked off his scholarship-funded stay because of those screams, screams like these ones, empty of fear or indignation – shrieks that asked for, begged for, mercy.

He got up from his new bed, Niurka's living room sofa, and walked along the hallway to his aunt's room, navigating like a bat by the sound of her screams in the darkness. He opened the door and found her lying rigid, faceup, with her fists and eyelids closed with a force that had nothing to do with rest. A bit of frothy saliva could be seen at the corner of her mouth. The full moon cast stripes from the window's security bars onto the sheets. Down the street, a motorist was dragging cans tied onto his *concho* to celebrate the inauguration of the Dominican Liberation Party, his father's party. It was the same technique baseball fans used to celebrate their champions.

With a forced delicacy that did not come naturally to him, he shook his aunt by the shoulder. "Aunt Niurka," he said, "it's just a nightmare." She opened her eyes and let out one last scream, much softer now. She got up, slowly and quietly. "You were screaming," Argenis told her. "Are you OK?" "I'm great," she said, using her feet to search for her slippers without turning on the lamp. She threw the sheet over herself, flattening down her rounded shrub of frizzy hair, and walked to the kitchen with Argenis following behind. She took a bottle of Barceló Imperial rum from the cabinet like it was a gallon of milk for breakfast, turned on the kitchen's light bulb, and poured two glasses. Argenis emptied his without waiting for her, and then she did the same, looking him in the eye for the first time.

"What were you dreaming about?" Argenis asked. "The same thing as always," she responded, downing a second glass to smooth the furrows the screams, tractor-like, had left in her voice. "And what is it that you see?" She opened a button on her housedress and pulled her left breast out. A tit without a nipple. A few seconds were enough for the diagonal scar over her areola to be burned into her nephew's retina, for him to see its centipede shape projected on the walls for many minutes after she had covered the breast again.

Argenis downed a second glass, feeling the heavy atmosphere of the hour of intimate revelations closing over his head. Involuntary, stuttering images of what he felt sure Niurka was about to tell him rolled through his head like an abstract trailer for a horror film.

"I wasn't a communist or anything. Your dad was always the hothead. But he has the luck of the devil, and after the purges of 1971 they weren't able to catch him again. I used to collect the pictures of the martyrs that came out in the paper: Orlando Martínez, El Moreno, Tingó. Like picture postcards. I liked to look at them there in the shoebox. They were dead and I was alive. Alive with all my secrets inside, secrets that had nothing to do with Balaguer or with

Castro. They were asking for it, as Renata used to say. They wanted to die. They went around in the streets tempting the devil with their slogans and planning attacks that never amounted to anything. The rebels were a bunch of amateurs, but Balaguer's assassins were professionals. They'd take you down just for having a university degree. I didn't want to overthrow any government. What I wanted was to go out dancing, but José Alfredo wouldn't even let me listen to music in English. That fucking man only started listening to the Beatles in the eighties because Tony Catrain played them for him. If it wasn't for Tony, he'd still be listening to Niní Cáffaro."

Niurka smiled sadly as she said "Cáffaro" and put her hand on her pajama just where her breast was, for a second, as if shutting a folder with a click. Then she poured herself a third drink, looked at the contents of the glass, and tossed it down her throat like a bucket of dirty water onto the street. Argenis breathed a sigh of relief, sensing that the story of the tit had been put off for another night. He couldn't allow a woman to beat him at drinking, though, so he imitated his aunt's move with a last drink, even though the two previous ones were already scratching up his insides. The clock that hung above the picture window showed four a.m. Niurka stood up and walked toward her room, turned off the main lights, and without looking at him said, "Go and lie down – take advantage of the few hours you have left."

"The few hours I have left," Argenis repeated in a loud voice, tossing himself onto the IKEA sofa bed with his head at the foot and his feet on the cushions, adding, "Sounds like a death sentence," although his aunt couldn't hear the joke. In that position, thanks to the light from the street, he could see the photos Niurka had hung on the wall over the sofa. Niurka at her first communion, with her frizzy hair smoothed out under the white veil and her gray eyes that were really green. Niurka at her first birthday, with Don Emilio and Milito next to a cake in the shape of a horseshoe. Niurka all bundled up and happy, in the Retiro Park in Madrid in the early eighties. Niurka's mom, his grandma Consuelo, on the patio of Renata and Emilio's house, where she worked, laughing about something to the photographer, her hair now gray, wearing the light-blue servant's uniform that neither Niurka nor José Alfredo had managed to get her out of.

On the other walls hung prints by Bidó that Niurka had inherited from Renata and some laminated fliers for concerts at Casa de Teatro. Next to the entry was a framed vinyl LP of the Beatles and, above the doorway, a little rag doll dressed in an outfit of denim jacket and jeans. She had brought the furniture over from her apartment in Spain, and she had just bought the stereo system – the best thing in the house – in Plaza Lama, along with the ceiling fans and the refrigerator.

Looking at the photos and the house, one might think that his aunt was and had been happy. But now, the centipede on her breast was superimposed on that landscape. Why had no one ever spoken of that breast? Did everyone else know that Niurka's nipple was missing? Did they know her screams could be heard down Bolívar Avenue at night?

It was clear that he was wide awake, and that his wakefulness would swallow up the few hours left to him like his aunt had swallowed the rum from the cupboard. He went over to the bookshelf in search of something to do. Turning on the reading lamp next to the sofa, he found a dress hanging from one of the shelves on a plastic-covered hanger, the kind that comes from a dry cleaner or a tailor shop. The outfit was green and red and as he got closer he could see that its skirt was made up of strips, like a Spartan soldier's. He lifted the plastic and confirmed that it was some kind of costume, a soldier's outfit, or an angel's. A sword and some sandals lay on the floor next to it. The sword was golden and said TOLEDO on the hilt. The sandals were made of rustic leather, with long straps, the kind that crisscross the shin. Argenis had first seen them in a picture a very long time ago, along with the rest of the outfit.

He would have been about three or four and he was paying his obligatory Sunday visit to Renata and Emilio's house, where his grandmother was still a servant. His brother Ernesto was Don Emilio's favorite, and his father's, too. José Alfredo had prepared some questions about recent Dominican history – the April Revolution, the Mirabal sisters, Orlando Martínez – which Ernesto answered eloquently, to the delight of Don Emilio. Meanwhile, Argenis slipped away to his grandmother's room, a dark, damp room whose only light entered through a square foot of window that looked out onto the street and was covered by a Persian blind.

There, on top of a little table lit by a candle, coconut and sweet-potato candies and bottles of carbonated beverages sat in front of a picture of Archangel San Miguel, who presided over the table with his sword, his scale, and a headful of blond ringlets. Beneath the angel's feet lay a black man with horns and claws who seemed to be part of the very earth, which was also black and aflame. The angel was about to split the head of that man with his sword, an eternal threat that would never come to pass.

Hypnotized by the atmosphere of that cave of unpainted walls, of mirrors under the bed, of sharpened corks that floated in a gourd bowl full of water, of colorful handkerchiefs tied to a chair, of bottles filled with herbs, of woven threads under the pillow, of sandals laid out in the shape of a cross, of bitter smells, half-smoked cigars, bells, and plastic saints, Argenis had reached for the sweets and a bottle of soda. The candies were rancid and the soda was warm. He returned the half-nibbled candy to its place and took a second sip to unstick the burnt sugar from his molars. Consuelo entered unannounced and dragged him out to the patio by one ear. "Damned boy! That belongs to Belié." "Don't tell Papi, Mamina," he begged his grandmother, with crumbs of coconut still stuck to his lips. She felt sorry for him and hugged him to her small breasts that smelled of pine-tar soap. The old candy and the soda began to take effect and Argenis got an attack of cramps. They laid him down in the room that had first been Milito's and then Niurka's before she left on scholarship for Spain.

In the eighties, Niurka would return every other year with the nurses from the psychiatric hospital where she worked, and on these trips they would rent the house of Tony Catrain, José Alfredo's best friend, in Las Terrenas. It was a three-bedroom, alpine-style cabin on the idyllic and solitary Playa Bonita. His dad would drive him and Ernesto there to see their aunt while Etelvina remained at work in the capital, thus giving José Alfredo space to enjoy the Spanish women who sunbathed in the nude in front of the house by day, and went with him into the dark water by night, none of them checking if the children had already gone to bed.

Argenis picked up the sword and found it was no toy. It was heavy and as sharp as a razor blade. He thrust it into a shadow in his mind, a shadow made of ocher stains that gradually grew more and more defined, like a Polaroid. It was his father, with no protection against the sword other than the grotesque jowls that were gaining terrain in the photos of him that appeared in the papers.

You are getting older and uglier every day and I bet you can't even get it up anymore, Argenis thought, as he tried out a series of movements with the weapon. He repeated the detailed choreography several times as the outer world began to fill up with the noise of motorcycle taxis and male voices announcing the destinations of the *conchos* and minibuses. The sound of his aunt in the shower interrupted him and, as he returned the sword to its place, the golden detailing around the neck of the costume caught the first light of day and attracted his gaze. In a few seconds he had made a mental list of the paints and brushes he would need to reproduce on canvas the effect of the light hitting the sequins. The pictorial recipe came to him like a reflex, a side effect of his artistic education.

When Niurka came out of the bathroom, Argenis had breakfast ready for her: toast, eggs over hard, and coffee. Along with a few questions. She was wearing a short linen dress with red and white stripes, and had gathered her hair into a bun. With no Afro to compete with, her green eyes gathered up all the light in the room. He had already eaten and was looking through the yellow pages for Orestes Loudón's tailor shop. "What are you looking for?" she asked, spreading orange marmalade onto a piece of toast. "A tailor," he replied, tearing the page from the phone book and sticking it in his pocket. "You've never been one to go around in suits," she said as she took too big a bite. "There's a first time for everything," he said, glancing over at the San Miguel costume that had sparked his curiosity, postponing his questions about it for another time and getting up to put another pot of coffee on the stove.

"The park," Argenis requested, handing the coins for his fare to the driver of the *concho*. Without turning his small head, the man took the payment with a hand extended backwards, taking advantage of the red light to tell someone on the other end of his cell phone call to put six eggs on to boil and get a couple of rolls ready.

Argenis imagined the woman on the other end of the line peeling the hard-boiled eggs and mashing them with salt and oil until they turned into a bright yellow paste that she'd spread on a couple of white rolls recently delivered from the *colmado*. The imagined scent made him hungry, but the various stenches with which passengers had cured the vinyl of the car seats were much stronger.

The door was missing its window pane and Argenis stuck his head out to breathe some fresh air, but outside it smelled like spoiled milk, and like the bitter, liquid scent of rotting vegetables. It smelled of human shit, of layers of sooty sweat, of the dust raised by Haitian workers' drills. It smelled like dead rats, like a congregation of sick pigeons, like a drunk's vomit, and of the green stew of water that had been standing in the ditches for months and months. The woman on the other end of the call scraped a layer off this mixture with her knife, like scraping a stick of butter. Argenis could see pieces of human fingers with dirty nails compacted inside that stick, and then the driver scarfing the disgusting sandwich down into a nearly toothless mouth.

"Artistic ability," Professor Herman had called the involuntary ease with which her student mixed reality and invention, repeating it to calm him when, three years ago now, she had come to the mental health ward of the UCE to bring him books and cigarettes. She had pulled these gifts from a Hermès bag, smiling behind her huge, expensive sunglasses. Now that the Dominican Liberation Party had won, she would soon be named director of the Museum of Modern Art. Her training and career meant she deserved the post, but they would have given it to her even if she were illiterate, just because of her mother's position in the party.

As he got out of the car in front of Independence Cemetery and looked through the iron gate, Argenis saw a chubby woman lighting a black candle placed next to a blackened pot of rice and beans on top of a tomb. Behind her, two fifty-something mulatto men held the same color candles and prayed, eyes closed, shirts stained with sweat. The woman caught Argenis's gaze, raising her eyebrows like she would raise her arms to challenge an opponent in a street fight. Then she brought a bottle of gin to her mouth, took a swig, and blew, spraying it over the food they were offering to the Baron of the Cemetery. Under the rays of the sun the atomized liquid momentarily formed a little rainbow in the air. The red plastic Casio watch Niurka had given him showed it was noon; vendors were crowding around outside the cemetery to sell their dusty lottery tickets.

Susana had warned him on that Havana balcony that the only thing that had changed since the Middle Ages was technology. Worldly flesh continued to be imprisoned by the same old superstitions. Next to the cemetery gate, old men and women besieged the vendors with money in their hands, requesting specific numbers they had dreamed the night before. A black dog was number four, a motorcycle taxi was a two.

The light of the white-hot sun left nothing to the imagination. The pockmarked walls and the impressive rust on gates and gutters surfaced like lines of text highlighted by a fluorescent marker. When he got to the Padre Billini Hospital, Argenis was sweaty from head to foot and for the first time he thought that maybe this wasn't a good idea. Next to the entrance to the hospital, red plastic bags were piled in a heap as tall as him – red because they contained organic waste, bloody gauze, and used syringes. The mountain of trash emitted the same disagreeable energy as the queue of patients next to it, waiting their turn for a consultation or for the delivery of some medicine. They all looked terminally ill, and some were praying. The line reached all the way to the corner, and there on the corner was the store at which, twenty years earlier, his dad had revealed the mysteries of Christmas.

Inside, the son of the man from Baní who had waited on them that day was preparing Cuban sandwiches to add to his wares. Argenis had to commemorate the return of the hateful memory, so he ordered the same thing his dad had way back then: a small bottle of rum and a Pepsi, which he mixed in a Styrofoam cup with ice and half a lime. He was getting good at making Cuba libres, and this one slid down his throat like an ocean breeze. Without stepping out of the shade of the store's eaves projecting over the sidewalk, he checked out the latest-model SUVs that were parked outside Orestes Loudón's tailor shop across the street, and decided to cross, netting a three-point shot with the empty cup into a nearby trash can. The drivers waiting for their bosses, wetting their Doritos with red sodas, watched as he walked in unannounced.

Just inside the door, they had added an Italian sofa, on which the owners of the SUVs were waiting to be attended. This little waiting room was now divided from the workshop by a heavy crimson curtain. The walls, which before had been bare, were now painted in a creamy biscuit color that failed to hide the hundred-year-old cracks in the Spanish masonry. Behind the sofa hung an enormous painting by some Guillo Pérez imitator. Argenis thought it was horrible. He pulled back the curtain and once more saw the table covered in rolls and snippets of cloth at the back of the shop and a flat-screen television on which two of Loudón's helpers were watching *La Opción de las 12* while sewing on their respective machines. The door to the little room beside it, where Loudón took his measurements, was closed. The assistants turned to look at him and then each other, before going back to their comedy show. He couldn't understand why the tailor hadn't taken advantage of his success to get out of that place; it still looked like a dungeon, even dressed up with expensive-looking objects.

Argenis could smell cigarette smoke coming from behind the door. When he opened it, the tailor smiled and, recognizing the jacket he'd made for Bebo and which Argenis now wore, reached his dark fingers out toward the lapel, smoothly taking it from him. "Never wear another man's clothes," he said, pausing a second at the sweat stain on the collar as he put the jacket on a hanger and hung it from the handle of a Persian blind.

"I thought you'd never come," Loudón mused, offering Argenis a chair across from his sewing machine, a white plastic chair like the thousands that had, with their geriatric, potty-seat appearance, superseded artisanal wicker chairs of woven palm fronds. The tailor was wearing a red polo shirt and black pants, and thanks to the polo he looked younger than he had in the eighties. The rigid little mustache was still in place and he kept his nails spotless, though, like a guitar player's, they were a few millimeters longer than was usual. Argenis silently wondered, Does he really remember me? and Loudón responded, "You look just like your dad, but you have a better build and color, because José Alfredo is dark-skinned, and fat besides."

For months he had been silently cursing his father, calling him a cocksucker out loud when no one could hear him, but when Argenis heard the other man insulting José Alfredo he felt bad and wanted to defend him. "Genes are everything," Loudón jabbered on from the other side of the machine as he lit another cigarette from the butt of the previous one. "You know they can get your DNA off that disgusting collar," he said, pursing his lips toward Bebo's jacket, and then, blowing smoke through his nose, he added, "One goes around leaving bits of oneself all over. Keep that in mind if you're going to kill someone." And his laughter, which burst out without warning, was sharp and mocking, like that of a shameless old whore.

When he saw Loudón get out of his seat and grab a yellow measuring tape that hung with a few others on the back of his chair, Argenis opened his mouth: "I want a suit." "Why else would you have come?" Loudón said, gesturing for him to get up as he opened an old, battered school notebook. Without asking his name, Loudón wrote "Argenis Luna Durán" with a red Paper Mate at the top of a page before sticking his arms out like Christ on the cross so that Argenis would do the same. Then, without using his hands to smoke the cigarette between his lips, the tailor proceeded to take his new client's measurements. After each measurement Loudón wrote the result down next to the body part.

From the neck to the shoulder, so much.

The chest, so much.

The waist, so much.

Shoulder to shoulder, the width of the back.

From neck to waist, from shoulder to wrist, the circumference of the wrist.

The length and circumference of the arm.

The hips.

The length of the leg.

From the waist to the groin and from the groin down the length of the leg again.

Using these measurements, Loudón would cut patterns like the ones he had tacked up on the door and then he'd use them to cut out the selected fabric. Those tissue paper patterns reminded Argenis of the flayed hide of a cow – shadows snipped by scissors, just as light casts shadows from a body onto a wall. With those shadows, the tailor would work his miracle on the basis of his clients' tastes and aspirations.

After closing the notebook Loudón bent over a pile of magazines and pulled one out. He flipped through it and showed two pictures to Argenis. The first portrayed a male model in a navy-blue sports coat with gold buttons, one hand resting on the sail of a catamaran; in the second an older man crossed a European street in a formal black suit. Argenis chose the second.

"What is this suit for?" Loudón asked him as he stubbed out the cigarette on the sole of his shoe and tossed it out the window. For a second Argenis thought of telling the truth: "To take revenge on my father, to make him feel guilty, so he'll pay what he owes me." He knew he would go to visit him, elegantly dressed, but he wasn't too clear on the details of his plan.

He asked the tailor, "How much will it cost?"

"Your dad has brought in a lot of people, good clients, so this one's on the house."

Orestes Loudón accompanied him to the waiting room where his other clients were grumbling, though he didn't appear to notice. When they reached the doorway he pinched one of Argenis's cheeks as one does a child's and then suddenly completed his caress by pulling out a couple of facial hairs. Argenis jumped back in pain and the tailor, looking at the black hairs between his fingers, said, "Come back Friday and do me the favor of throwing out the beggar's clothing you have on."

He was thirsty. As he calculated what a Presidente might now cost at Luis's bar, someone yelled his name and honked a horn three times. Argenis turned around to look and recognized Charlie Catrain, his bosom buddy, in a Nissan Xterra with a longboard on the rack. "Get in, man!" Charlie requested, lowering his window and pouring a welcome blast of air-conditioning onto the sidewalk and onto Argenis.

Before the smoke coming out of his mouth could dissipate, Charlie passed the bong to Argenis for him to light the weed in the bowl and take a drag. The lighter had a woman with huge, pink breasts printed on it and the water in the bong's base made a blub, blub, blub sound. In the background, the album "Nice Guys" by Art Ensemble of Chicago was spinning on Charlie Catrain's record player. Next to the record player, on a polished teak table, sat some other analogue devices from the seventies. Opposite it a stone Buddha's head was smiling stupidly.

He had known Charlie his whole life. Charlie's dad, Tony Catrain, and Argenis's father had sent them both to Cuba for the first Latin American Communist Youth Conference, a kind of summer camp whose slogan was "Be Like Che." The food tasted like shit, and the discussions about the new color for the pioneers' berets were a drag. The female hosts, however, were really hot, and they were in charge of the afternoon swimming lessons in the pool. One of those afternoons Charlie took him to an empty building in the camp complex and there, on a stinking mat, he made him lose his virginity to a girl from Matanzas who was very thin and pale, and who he had convinced to open her legs for a package of nail polish which Charlie's mother had made him pack as a gift for his female revolutionary friends. Argenis stuck

106

his dick into that bony pussy and came without thrusting even once. Then Charlie, with the bag of colorful polish in his hand, made the girl suck him off on her knees, telling Argenis, "Next time think of your grandma so you won't come so soon, *maricón*."

"So what's your plan?" his friend was now asking, as Argenis remembered Charlie's juvenile penis decorating the Cuban girl's face with spiderwebs of semen like a Halloween skull. Waiting for a response, Charlie took off his shoes and passed the bong to Argenis again, as if to encourage him.

"I have a plan," Argenis said at last, dry-coughing from the weed.

"What is it?" Charlie asked again, getting up from the L-shaped white sofa on which, from time to time, he'd still pay for someone to suck him off.

Argenis took the bong and inhaled as he kept up his own old habit of answering questions only in his mind. Charlie went over to the kitchen table, combing through his black curls with his fingers, and took a ball of cocaine the size of a baby's fist out of a little wooden box. The bleachy smell of the cocaine ran all the way down into Argenis's guts. He could already taste the line he would soon be snorting when Charlie passed him his American Express card, in an invitation to use it like a razor blade.

Charlie again sat down beside him, barefoot, but with his pearl-gray Hugo Boss suit pants and blood-red tie still in place. A few minutes earlier, he had balled up his jacket as he entered the apartment and tossed it onto the dining room table. Argenis supposed he must have more than enough of them, given all the care he'd taken to crumple it up. Unlike his father – how he had cared for the first suit Loudón had ever made him! Whenever he'd come in off the street he would immediately remove it and hang it up on the balcony to air out, then walk through the house in his underwear asking if dinner was ready, while his mom silently smashed green plantains with an aluminum cup under the yellow kitchen light.

Argenis chopped the coke with the edge of the card, making two lines for himself and two for Charlie on the glass coffee table. Charlie used a rolled up thousand-peso bill to inhale the unadulterated drug he'd got through some Venezuelan friends of his father's. Tony Catrain was the black sheep of a wealthy family of lawyers. He had studied in Italy and come back to Santo Domingo in 1972 to enjoy the company of the Dominican political and artistic avant-garde, who he entertained every weekend at his house in Las Terrenas. The house was deserted in those days, making it both ideal for social experiments and invisible to Balaguer and his henchmen. At the time of his revolutionary splendor José Alfredo had impressed him, but in the eighties Tony had dumped him, resuming a friendship based on mutual interests when José Alfredo had been installed in the National Palace together with his party.

Charlie had taken a doctorate in international law, but like his father he now defended corrupt politicians of all parties. Charlie was twenty-seven, like Argenis, and he had a son with a Chilean ex; a photo of the boy in Valparaiso, wearing a soccer kit, was stuck on the fridge with a magnet that was also a bottle opener. Charlie'd had no trouble turning into a charming version of his own father. He looked satisfied and tranquil. Argenis, on the other hand, had long been fighting against the irritating resemblance the mirror cast back at him, and he thought that he had done everything up to that point only to sully that reflection, to cover the face of his father with stains, to disfigure it with failures. When he was little, he had been proud of that

108

resemblance – it was the only thing he had on his brother Ernesto, who had their mother's light hair and skin.

At some point after that first, long-ago visit to the tailor, when the two of them had looked into the mirror in Loudón's shop, his father all dressed up and he himself saying a final goodbye to jingle bells, he began to hate that face, to hate those familiar gestures.

A few hours later, the kitchen table had turned into a modest laboratory, covered with smoking pipes, Ziplocs full of hydroponic marijuana, pills, and lines of coke belonging to Charlie's guests, ex-students from the progressive school Argenis had attended as a child, as well as children of members of the party who had just won the election, like him. Dioradna and Fifo were no longer those Greenpeace members soliciting signatures on El Conde Street: now they were bureaucrats who preferred to talk contemporary art rather than politics. The suffocating competition between various brand-name fragrances hung in the air. They didn't know or pretended not to know about the crossroads at which Argenis stood, and they asked him about his art, his paintings, the next exhibition, as if nothing had happened since he graduated from Chavón. They were the spitting image of their progenitors, but without the ideological baggage their parents had used to plan attacks. They looked contented, not at all naive, grateful for the battles their parents had fought against Trujillo and Balaguer but lacking any interest in perpetuating the struggle. They knew the reason for their current solvency. It had nothing to do with education or progress – all the plenty was the product of a pact. The PLD had made a pact with Balaguer and won the elections for the first time ever in 1996. In a final sacrifice for their country, their parents had signed a deal with the murderer of their comrades. Thankful for their privileges, free of contradictions and excuses, this was the new Dominican nobility.

A strangely good mood sank into his bones and he lied with very specific details about an exhibition that he had been preparing for months. In his mind's eye he saw the pieces in that exhibition already finished and hung in a large, well-lit gallery, along with the reviews in the papers and the orange stickers with the word SOLD stuck just next to the pieces. The table paid him the kind of attention Argenis hadn't received in years and he felt something inside him start to let go, to relax, to get comfortable with the inherited resemblance which sat so easily with his companions, to take advantage of his genetic circumstances: looking like his old man, being like him.

He opened his eyes on Charlie's sofa, a designer sofa he was afraid he'd drooled or sweated on. Charlie served him some toast and coffee in the kitchen before dropping Argenis at his Aunt Niurka's house on his way to work. It was summer and there were no parents blasting their car horns on the way to their children's schools. Under the morning light the scars that population growth had left on Santo Domingo looked less aggressive, like grime on a peacefully sleeping beggar. Argenis's head hurt a bit when he got out of the car. He said goodbye, and from the gate of the building's parking lot he saw his mother pressing the intercom button to go up and see him at Niurka's place. He had asked Niurka not to say anything to Etelvina yet, but the request had been in vain. He hid behind the wall and took a second to calculate the effects the rough night had had on his appearance. Mami will think I'm shooting up, he thought as he went down the street, shaking his head to empty it of the guilt he felt at leaving Etelvina there, dreaming of seeing him, ringing the bell of an empty apartment.

He walked as far as Máximo Gómez to kill time, bought a coffee from the thermos of a *paletero* selling frozen treats and sat down on a low wall outside the Supermercado Nacional. He was still running from his mother's gaze, like a teenager. He didn't want to hurt her anymore, he didn't want to deceive her. But he also didn't want to answer her questions about Cuba. What could he tell her about? Susana? Bengoa? Vantroi? Now that he really thought about it, though, she wasn't going to ask him about the past. The only thing that mattered to her was the future: what plans he had, how he'd make a living, whether he'd go look for work the next day. He went into the supermarket. He had a few pesos left from what he'd taken from Bebo. He bought milk, passion fruit juice, and a few plantains. On the way to Niurka's he stopped twice to fix his shirt in a car window and to confirm that the bags under his eyes were not as big as he'd thought. When he got to the parking lot he found Etelvina leaning on the hood of her car, talking on her cheap little cell phone. When she saw him, she hung up without saying goodbye and walked toward him with open arms. He put the supermarket bags on the ground in order to return her hug, happy with the effect his little bit of theater had had on her.

"*Mijo*, how handsome you look," she said, her eyes tearful, still holding on to his arm as they climbed the stairs.

"Thanks, Mami. You look really good, too," he said, and kissed her head. In reality, he thought she looked much older. New and deeper wrinkles, for which he felt responsible, had appeared by her eyes and mouth.

Now, in Niurka's apartment, they put on the coffee and drank it while eating some garlic *casabe*, as Argenis recounted some anecdotes about Cuba's general poverty. His mother had abandoned all her Castroist dreams long ago, one of the many dreams that had died during her relationship with José Alfredo Luna.

Etelvina believed in nothing and he had only seen her praying once. It was 1987, and against all predictions Balaguer was president once again. Bundled up against the strange Caribbean cold of the start of the year, fathers, mothers, grandparents, and children were all waiting their turn in the annual Epiphany toy handout at the president's house. His mother had asked him to go with her, because this year they were going to give out sewing machines to the first 500 mothers in line. His father cursed it as "disgusting Balaguerist alms," so they agreed not to tell him.

Etelvina was praying she wouldn't be seen; not by her friends, or her leftist ex-friends, not by anyone. The line was long – it reached all the way to the National Theater, even though the sun wasn't yet up. Every year, there were injuries. Mothers who came to blows over a bicycle, old men capable of poking each others' eyes out to grab a rubber baby doll, children who were crying because they only got an inflatable beach ball. Argenis and Ernesto didn't want toys anymore: they asked Etelvina for clothes, brand-name sneakers, cash; things that she would get for them by saving up the little extra money she got from tutoring. Her schoolteacher's salary was only enough for what was absolutely necessary. She had been promised a position as a professor in the Autonomous University, and although she didn't believe in anything, she prayed that she would get it, as she waited in this line that smelled of the fried salami sold on the sidewalk.

"They're Singer machines, good ones," a friend had told her, because Etelvina had mentioned that during her childhood in La Vega she helped her mother sew pajamas and nightgowns for children, curtains and pillowcases, simple things that they would sell in her father's *colmado*. She remembered her embroidered name on the little labels her mother put into the necklines, like a brand. ETELVINA, the label read. Etelvina hated her name. A damned ugly name. Etelvina was a servant's name, an illiterate's name. It was a

113

name that bestowed on her everything Etelvina wanted to cleanse from the world: poverty, ignorance, filth. Argenis was convinced that in spite of her militant Marxist past she hated the poor. She hated them for their bare, worm-catching feet, for their rags, and for the X they had used to sign their bills in her dad's shop in her childhood.

Argenis's grandfather, a Spanish republican who had gone into exile in 1937, had taught her to read and add when she was just five. He'd also explained to her some things about a man named Marx, and she had understood. These people, hardened by poverty and resignation, people who came to them to buy a pound of sugar and bottle of oil on credit, would one day have enough water to bathe in, to brush their teeth. Those monsters who smiled with rotten teeth and bloody gums, those with chewed, greenish nails and rounded, calloused fingers, with skeletal calves, purplish from the leeches in the rice fields, had to be educated so that they could escape from the yoke of their oppressors. Socialism smelled of laundry soap and new textbooks. It was the magic potion against the ugliness of the world. Not against injustice, but against the aesthetic inequality of men.

Around nine in the morning the doors of Balaguer's house opened and total chaos ran down the line along with the news. A policeman dragged a young pickpocket who had tried to take an older woman's purse onto the sidewalk across the street. He was jabbing his baton into the boy's ribs and the people were yelling "Kick his ass," and things like that.

Argenis then counted how many women were in front of them, omitting the children, men, and old folks, in order to calculate the probability his mother had of getting a sewing machine. He noticed Etelvina was praying again, this time to get one of them. They could see the first few lucky ones walking away with dolls, basketballs, and plastic machine guns. A very tall man was happily carrying a tiny blue bicycle, a teenager – childishly holding the hand of her albino grandfather – carrying a gigantic kitchen set, and behind her an older woman, black as night and assisted by two grandchildren with shaved heads, was carrying a sewing machine with the word BALAGUER printed on its little drawer. It was the kind that needed no electricity, with a metal pedal and a varnished wooden table. It was the same kind Etelvina's mother had used in La Vega.

A gentle murmur came down the line and then the shout of "They're giving out machines!" unzipped the precarious order the police had been trying to impose for hours. A stampede of creatures in skirts, hair rollers, heels, and housedresses came down Máximo Gómez Avenue, dumping babies into strangers' arms, pulling off shoes, swearing, and giggling as they made their way toward the truck from which they were unloading the president's glorious SINGER machines.

Infected with the euphoria, Argenis and Etelvina had run and pushed their way up to within a few meters from the truck's open mouth, where three men drenched in sweat lowered machines toward the whirlpool of arms, toward the agitated, ferocious heads of an agglomeration of bodies that pushed to occupy the same space. With a few strides and his six-foot height, Papi would have snatched the Singer from the hands of these men, Argenis thought, just before a fist in his stomach knocked the wind out of him. The pain didn't last long, anaesthetized as he was by rage. He elbowed his way through the crowd, crying, until he managed to get close to his mother again, her hair now falling out of her neat bun and her arms covered in scratches. She was alone and it didn't matter if they saw her, her friends, her ex-comrades – they were all a bunch of shit-eaters.

She wanted that machine to make a few extra pesos, to save for her children's college education, to shove it in José Alfredo's face and say, "Even Balaguer does more for this household than you. You shit, you freeloader, you thief; parasite, scoundrel, jerk." Argenis raised his delicate hands so they could pass him one, but the constant motion of the whirlpool dumped him on his ass next to his mother at the edge of the riot. Etelvina stood up once more to throw herself, eyes closed, into the vortex, but a hand on her shoulder stopped her, the hand of an elegant mulatto offering her water in a little plastic cup. Asking no questions – he had seen it all – the man led them to the front end of the truck, which was cordoned off by black-helmeted police and a metal barricade. Argenis was sure that what had saved them was the fact that his mother was white; white and pretty. A woman with dyed orange hair motioned for them to pass. The woman was wearing a red T-shirt with the party logo on it. It read, LO QUE DIGA BALAGUER, "Whatever Balaguer Says," in letters deformed by her obesity. "Are you for Balaguer?" she asked Etelvina, passing her a form on which she was supposed to write down her name, identification number, and address. Argenis saw how Etelvina's hands were trembling as she signed the paper resting on her new machine and how her writing, always so neat and straight, came out as ugly as one of her second-grade students' on that piece of paper.

That day's human blender had disheveled her insides. It was almost twenty years ago and Argenis was sure that the Etelvina of today, the one that wouldn't take shit from anyone, had been born in that line. The experience had also solidified a link they had always had, one his mother didn't share with anyone else. He really loved her, and now that he saw her aging before his eyes, even as she sipped her coffee as noisily as ever, that love hurt him a little. Before they said their farewells, while she was writing down Ernesto's work address on one of the Post-its Niurka had piled up next to the telephone, Argenis understood that some of his talent for drawing came from the capital letters with which his mother decorated the beginnings of her sentences and proper nouns.

"Go see your brother," she requested, and authoritatively stuck the little paper into his shirt pocket.

"Why did you come? To ask Dad for money? To worry Mom? You were in bad shape over there, doing your junkie thing. Like always. Embarrassing us. Dad stopped sending money because the Cuban intelligence agency called to tell him that Bengoa was giving you drugs. So you're an idiot, then? Fucking stupid. Retarded. You think Dad has no friends? Dad has friends everywhere, you imbecile. Why is it so hard for you to do what's right? Does nothing matter to you? 'Fuck Dad, let him lose his position in the party, let Mom die of worry. Just let them die.' Right? That's what you want – for them to rot. Two heroes who went through all kinds of horror for this country of ingrates, just so you can come back and make things hard for them. Piece of shit."

Ernesto never stopped. Dressed in a mustard-colored Prada suit that was too small for him, he was cleaning his nails with the tip of a letter opener as he spoke. He said the words without anger, with a feigned delicacy, as if he were talking to a little girl, his feet up on a desk covered in folders and papers.

Argenis didn't know how his brother paid for this office full of Le Corbusier furniture, with picture windows looking out on Naco and Piantini. On its walls hung minimalist drawings by some current Dominican artist, some ex-schoolmate of his from Fine Arts, some lucky asshole with much less talent than he had. How much had Ernesto paid for each drawing, he wondered, dropping himself onto the metal skeleton of one of the armchairs.

Ernesto broke off his attack to take a call and Argenis moved on from the drawings to look at his older brother's shoes, which were black and pointy with a supernatural shine. They were there on the table for Argenis to kiss, for Argenis to caress the creased surface of their soles with his extended tongue, just as his brother had made him do when they were kids and Argenis had lost some bet. Because Ernesto always won their contests. He was the first to reach the top of the pine tree on the corner, and his green gobs of spit made it onto the neighbor's patio while Argenis's just hung there on their own blinds.

Ernesto was better at sports, better in school, better at everything. He knew how to say the things that made their father happy, something Argenis could never manage, no matter how hard he tried. Their father had taught Ernesto card tricks, had shown him old maps in the encyclopaedia and told him war stories that he never shared with Argenis. Their father also praised Ernesto in front of people: for his successes as a catcher in the baseball league, for his out-standing grades, for his even teeth, for the way he would sing Silvio Rodríguez's "Playa Girón" with tears in his eyes.

Argenis thought he could see the fruits of those envied moments in the ample pride that kept his brother's spine erect, his chin pointing out some spot on the horizon, his chest puffed out like a fighting cock's.

Ernesto got up from his enormous armchair, took three steps around to the front of the desk, and made a little backwards jump to sit on it. He was as white as their mother Etelvina, but had inherited their father's appetite: he was much shorter than Argenis and a spare tire was starting to encircle his midsection. His feet hung down like those of a plucked chicken and Argenis could see the colorful checked socks he wore under his pants. Ernesto swung his feet as he inspected his nails. "You know what this is?" he asked, putting one hand on top of the mountain of paper. "It's the future. Projects, investments, capital. Contracts we're giving to people. Investors who come to put money into your country. The president brought me from Argentina to evaluate them. You could have a slice of the pie, too, except that you're a retard."

Another call demanded Ernesto's attention and Argenis dared to serve himself a whiskey from the designer minibar in the corner. There he looked at himself in the mirror that covered the wall. He was wearing Bebo's brown pants and a cotton shirt his Aunt Niurka had given him. He didn't look so bad, except for the overly long toenails that peeked out from his leather sandals. In the background a man who shared his blood, wearing a designer suit too tight for him, was seducing one of his lovers in a loud voice.

A driving rain began to beat against the windows and Argenis imagined the scene as part of a Dominican musical. In it, his brother, wearing the designer suit and a Che-style starred beret, danced under a downpour of government contracts for building bridges, highways, and medical clinics. Ernesto shared his pie with other choreographed scoundrels, most of them fat and bald and in linen suits, who spun in place while smiling up at the sky from which a deluge of paper and liquid shit was falling. With sadistic pleasure, Argenis filled Ernesto's mouth with that shit until he was forced to swallow it, to savor it, with a smiling, stupid face.

An assistant had entered with lunch on a silver tray. Ernesto had ordered from some menu a half hour earlier. Without offering anything to Argenis, he went back to his chair and took the metal covers from the steaming plates. He placed the telephone next to the tray and turned it onto speaker. A flirtatious woman's voice on the other end asked about the color of some rugs. He cut the fish with knife and fork and put a huge piece into his mouth. His eyes gleamed with something empty and monstrous, like Saturn devouring his son in the Goya painting. Content in the belly of the Titan, he imitates his gestures, thought Argenis.

As he chewed, Ernesto took out his wallet and grabbed three or four thousand-peso bills. Argenis had just put the empty glass back in the corner minibar, and again he saw the mirror reflecting a pale man, marked by adolescent acne, pulling money from a wallet. He knew what was coming, but this time he was prepared. Ernesto offered him the pesos, speaking with his mouth full, but Argenis had already opened the door and was walking toward the exit on the way to the elevator. Spurned and angry, his older brother followed him to the lobby with fork in hand, and right there in front of the receptionist he said, "Mirta left you for a woman, didn't you know? Yes, Papito, a dyke stole her from you. A lesbo. She looks really happy going around with her dyke, and with a little boy who looks just like you."

He was already in the elevator when Ernesto said "just like you." The doors closed and the machine started its slow descent to the street. In his guts he felt the same pain he had felt in Havana when he quit using the synthetic morphine. Some absurd desire to vomit, even though he had nothing in his stomach, made him lean against the wall. When they separated, Mirta told him she had aborted a baby boy. His baby. And if that baby was alive? And he had a son? He felt panicked thinking about what was waiting for him down there, when at last the elevator doors opened. Suddenly everything gained an absolute and absorbing depth. The news of his successful reproduction had turned his world – a Paleochristian, naive, two-dimensional mural – into a Da Vinci painting, three-dimensional, wide-screen, in vivid perspective.

A line of taxis was waiting for customers at the exit of the office building. Inside the cars, dented eighties Japanese models, the drivers ate Chinese food over their newspaper or slept with the driver's seat in a horizontal position. Under a light-blue tarp tied to a *flamboyán* tree a street vendor sold cigarettes, sweets, and coffee from a rusty thermos. Argenis bought a pack of Nacionals and smoked one while looking at the pink waffle cookies on the cart, listening to the gravel-crunching sound of the taxi drivers' radios. The rain had stopped and an asphyxiating steam was rising from the asphalt. Niurka had given him a few pesos so he could get around, so he could look for work. His aunt had also loaned him a little pay-as-you-go cell phone, which she kept for foreign friends who came to visit her. He hailed a taxi and asked the driver to take him to the Mercado Modelo. On the way he dialed a number – one of the few he still knew by heart: Rambo, his heroin pusher.

Rambo was not in the habit of taking calls from unknown numbers, so he didn't hit redial. He calmed down as he anticipated the peace that soon, very soon, he would be feeling. Imagining the needle pushing it into him gave him goosebumps and filled his heart with a childlike euphoria. He avoided all thoughts of failure: that Rambo might have moved, that he wouldn't be home, that he could be traveling, or dead. He also avoided thinking about his Aunt Niurka and her good intentions, about the genuine affection she showed him, and about the offers of work she had made him. Giving art classes to abused women or to violent offenders wasn't his idea of happiness, but at the NGO where Niurka worked they could get him a studio and materials so that he could restart his career, once and for all.

Rambo lived on a street next to the market and Argenis, since he didn't really need the drugs, decided to walk to Little Haiti behind it before going up to knock on the door. When he was a student at Fine Arts he used to buy artifacts from other eras there for just a few pesos – used clothing a Haitian woman sold from a pickup, Ben Sherman shirts from the sixties, brightly colored polyester pants, even the motor from a remote-controlled car he had used to create a homemade tattooing machine. Most of these treasures came from the Duquesa dump. It was trash rescued by the dumpster divers who would later lay out the screws, picture frames, and faded plastic lunchboxes on a towel to sell.

This is the purgatory of all things, thought Argenis. Stuff that doesn't reach the heaven of antique shops and stuff that escapes the hell of Duquesa, here is where it all ends up. Maybe it's up to me to redeem one of them and elevate it to an eternal life in my bedroom. He felt generous and much calmer, and before getting to the end of the street where the dumpster divers had arranged their knickknacks, he proposed a stupid game to himself: if I find an object in the shape of a cat, it means I shouldn't shoot up. Renouncing all responsibility in this way, he already felt more optimistic. The cat thing was incidental; it was just the first animal that entered his head, and the occurrence brought to mind the little blue porcelain cat his mother had had in their home when he was little. His eyes skimmed over the edge of the sidewalk, stopping at pieces of iron, lead, and bronze of unknown origin, beach toys, ceramic plates, baskets, hardware, telephones, napkin holders, belts, forks with bent tines, and on top of a mountain of threadbare wigs, a black cat missing an eye. He picked it up to examine it.

The remaining eye was a plastic emerald. Around its neck it wore a collar of silvery lace from which hung a stone that matched the eye in shape but was ruby-red, and its velvet fur, although a bit bald in places, was shiny and very dark. It was a very old toy, maybe from the sixties. Maybe from the Trujillo era. He took out a fifty-peso bill without asking the price and handed it to the diver like he used to do back in the day; the guy put the money in his pocket without lifting his gaze from a steel apparatus he was trying to loosen with a screwdriver. As soon as the cat was his, Argenis forgot the deal he'd made with himself and walked with a quick step to Rambo's apartment. He pressed the animal to his chest and felt the hard stuffing inside it, either rice or sand, as he asked in a soft voice, "Little cat, little cat, who threw you in the trash? What sins could have kept you from reaching eternal glory?"

In twos, he went up the narrow steps of a stairway smelling of piss and beer. His friend's fourth-floor door sported a sticker from the last census and a deep groove made by some kind of blade. He pressed the bell and listened to the commotion of someone hiding whatever they could because they were always expecting the police. Rambo, an olive-toned mulatto, turned white as snow when he opened the door.

"Man, what you doing here? Get out of here, man. Leave me alone." Rambo was shitting himself with fear, and if Argenis hadn't stuck the cat between the door and its frame, he would have shut it in his face. With something like resignation in his sunken eyes he opened it again but didn't let Argenis enter. Behind him, a woman in an oversize T-shirt was lighting a cigarette from a stove burner in a dark kitchen.

"What's up, Rambo? You smoking crack? What kind of paranoia is this?"

"No paranoia, buddy," the pusher said, scratching his arms nervously with both hands. "Your dad came by with two thugs and stuck a Beretta in my mouth before sending you off to Cuba. I can't sell you anything, man. Get out of here. Don't call me. You don't know me, you never knew me, and I don't know you."

He had nothing left, not even a pusher. He flopped back onto Niurka's sofa bed and looked at the ceiling. He tried to remember the number of Hans, another pusher who had gotten heroin for him, but then he remembered Bebo had said Hans was in jail. Aunt Niurka is a psychiatrist, he thought. If I tell her, maybe she can get me some Valium, some lorazepam, something. In his mind he heard "priorities of a junkie," just the way his ex-wife used to say it. He went to the kitchen and served himself two shots of Barceló Imperial one after the other, returned to the sofa, lit a Nacional, and thought about how Susana had fucked Bengoa so that he could shit himself comfortably during his withdrawal syndrome. He thought about the son that, according to Ernesto, he might have, and again the memory of his grandmother came to him: Consuelo sitting on the bench in her bosses' kitchen, cleaning rice.

What was the meaning of that memory? Why was it always coming back, like a hip-hop loop? It was a living image, in color, which filled his nose with a mixture of smells that included the Vicks VapoRub Consuelo rubbed on her knees, the old wood of the cabinets, and the *sofrito* seasoning for the meat in the pot. He made an effort to recall more details, moving about inside the memory like in a virtual reality game, turning his head and walking around her house, traveling in time. He put out the cigarette, closed his eyes, and tried to relax. He voluntarily drew the image toward him: his grandmother Consuelo, not yet fifty years old back then. She had had his father very young. She is missing one of her first molars. Her long pianist's fingers delve into the rice, as if, instead of cleaning rice, she is picking the fleas from a dog. The space where her molar once was can be seen when she opens her mouth to say something. What is she saying?

Niurka's chaotic entrance with the supermarket shopping bags called him back to the present. He got up to help her, but she wouldn't let him, gesturing in the way he had seen his grandmother do before. Like help from others was an insult. He followed her to the kitchen and watched her put everything away as she shared the details of an amusing little drama at work with him. He took out the bag of weed Charlie had given him and showed it to his aunt, winking. She responded by passing him a book of cigarette papers that was lying on top of the refrigerator.

Argenis crumbled the contents of the packet on top of an old *National Geographic* magazine. A sunken treasure at some Caribbean port was on the cover. The underwater photo brought stories of pirates and dark curses to mind. After having thrown some spaghetti into boiling water, Niurka turned up the volume on the radio she had in the kitchen and "La Cima del Cielo" by Ricardo Montaner came on. His aunt was capable of enjoying Björk and Alvaro Torres back to back. If only I had such a capacity for joy, thought Argenis, laying the weed on the little paper path, rolling it with a single movement into a joint which he then sealed with the glue of a damp lick. They put it under a lamp to dry and sat down to eat in silence. Niurka ate slowly, as if it took great effort to select the combination of elements the fork would bring to her mouth, and from the corner of his eye Argenis looked at the San Miguel costume that hung from the shelf.

"It's your grandmother's," she said when she had finally finished her food, then added, "I suppose you'll inherit it," as they went up the stairs to the rooftop to light the joint.

"What do you mean, inherit?" asked Argenis.

"*Mijo*, misery inherits misery," she responded even more cryptically. Argenis took a deep drag and held his breath. When Niurka began to speak again he let the air and the smoke out slowly.

"Your grandmother serves the mysteries. She's San Miguel's horse. In our family, the youngest child inherits this condition. It was my turn, but I went off to Spain. I'd had enough already, what with being black, Dominican, and the daughter of a maid. Besides which I was also supposed to be a witch! The stuff of backward people. When I was little, Mami made me ring a bell to call the saint. Her eyes would roll back in her head and she'd speak with a different voice. It scared me."

Niurka told him these things in a tone somewhere between annoyed and comical. The street lights did not illuminate her face, but they made her African profile stand out. The glow at the tip of the joint lit up her features and for a second Argenis saw a *bruja*, the sorceress his aunt had never ceased to be. She had used the word "condition" to name that thing. It was obvious she thought Consuelo was a crackpot. Either that, or calling her crazy was her way of freeing herself from the spell. Argenis told Niurka that one day the old woman had fainted when they were visiting her at Emilio and Renata's house. It was in the days after the PLD's first triumph and his father was dressed very elegantly, showing the first hint of the sparkle that power would bring out of him. José Alfredo held her head and called out, "Mamá, Mamá." Renata brought her Bay Rum, the only time Argenis ever saw Renata do something for her servant. Consuelo was babbling something and his father turned his ear toward her to hear, then turned as pale as if he'd seen the dead, and crouched at her feet to rub them and get her circulation going. Later Argenis asked his dad what he had heard. José Alfredo pressed his lips together as if he were going to cry, and said, "Mujé salva gassó. Gassó traición mujé." Woman saves man, man betrays woman.

Consuelo didn't know that José Alfredo had left Etelvina. They'd hidden it from her so as not to worry her. What she did know was that one morning during Balaguer's twelve years Etelvina's brother, a marine, had saved both of them from being shot to death when he recognized them. That same day, Etelvina Durán and José Alfredo Luna married and abandoned the underground forever.

"San Miguel brings them," Niurka said in a weird voice, since she was holding the smoke in. Argenis thought of the suit and imagined himself wearing it. His aunt's voice made him laugh, and hearing him laugh made Niurka laugh. They laughed long, until they cried.

The street he knew was gone. Gone were the wide side-walks lined with jasmine, tamarind and almond trees, the modern houses built in 1950 by local architects who had recently returned from Mexico and Paris, the buildings made up of two or three apartments with high-ceilinged rooms and cool granite floors, the silence interrupted only by the calls of a passing street vendor and, from time to time, by student protests when they came off campus. Emilio's and Renata's was the only house on the block that hadn't yet been sold and carved up to accommodate low-rent shops. Microbusinesses stuffed into four square meters that announced their services in vulgar typefaces printed digitally onto vinyl banners. Color or black-and-white photocopies, internet cafés, and barber shops. Fake nails, Chinese cell phones, and second-hand clothing. Boarding houses for Haitian and Pakistani students, Serbian strippers, and male prostitutes. The dreaded slum that Renata had so often mentioned as a distant inconvenience had exploded right at the door of her house. But Renata was no longer there to complain, to send Consuelo to shut the French doors that opened onto the entry hall, because the street was full of nasty people; because, as Renata had yelled during her last weeks in the house, she had never seen so many ugly people in one place in all her life.

The doors that opened onto the street remained shut in spite of the definitive absence of the lady of the house, and Argenis had to bang on them with his fist several times before his grandmother came to ask "Who is it?" in a frail, frightened voice.

She couldn't hear over the megaphone of an evangelical preacher and the insistent speakers of the minibuses that came down from Correa y Cidrón Avenue, so she asked the same question three times before her grandson's answer reached her. The preacher's pickup truck went away along with its apocalyptic shouting and Consuelo, overjoyed by the visit, squealed like a girl. The wavering voice of a few seconds before now filled with vigor and a youthful scorn. Argenis heard her clanking around with a noisy key chain until she was finally able to open the door, a solid slab painted white, on whose surface one could still see the marks of the rocks Autonomous University students had thrown at the police during the conflicts of the seventies.

She had her habitual green handkerchief tied around her head so tightly that it looked like the knot was preventing a spill of some toxic substance. Although she was as skinny and wrinkled as a raisin, she always stood up straight and elegant.

The house was extremely tidy, just like her, and lit only by the doors that opened onto the courtyard. Argenis wondered if Consuelo still slept in the little servant's room out there, or if, now that Renata had left her the house, she slept in one of the family's bedrooms. Probably the woman was still attached to her monastic cell, as if any other space would cave in on her. A few pieces of hundred-year-old mahogany furniture had been reclaimed by Renata's sisters "for their sentimental value." Without the dining room table and the gigantic, mirrored armoire Argenis and Ernesto had hidden in as children, the space was even bigger and more extravagant for a single woman who still insisted on wearing her servant's uniform, even though her bosses only appeared in the two or three photos that still hung on the walls.

The television was on and the electronic music that signaled the beginning of the afternoon news streamed from it with a stubbornness like Consuelo's own, a stubbornness that Argenis interpreted as pride, the ascetic's sin. "See me here, virtuous and mortified," he imagined her saying, challenging God to find any desire in her, stubbornly covering herself with the infamous blue cloth she used to elevate herself above the material world she had always despised – or which, as Argenis thought, she had never understood.

The lights were off and Argenis dared to turn one on without asking permission, so that Consuelo could at last see the coconut and sweet-potato candies he had brought in a paper bag.

"Look. At. What. I. Have. Here," he said, raising his voice and enunciating each word. "They're sweets for your San Miguel."

"Be quiet, fool," she said, going into the kitchen to put the obligatory coffee pot on the stove. "You think I'm deaf or something?"

Argenis wondered if his grandmother's other faculties were in as good a shape as her hearing. She hadn't been possessed for ages. Her body had weakened, and she now suffered greatly with the visits of her saint: her nose bled, her bones hurt. Watching Consuelo refilling her empty sugar bowl at the back of that kitchen, Argenis thought that San Miguel had abused his horse, like those officers in the wars of independence who rode theirs until they dropped dead.

The smell of the sea came through the window. Its proximity had already rusted out a couple of Nedoca refrigerators and this latest one only shut when Consuelo put her old bench in front of it to block the door. That wooden bench with its rounded seat, where Consuelo had sat sideways for decades to clean rice, peel plantains, and listen to the radio while awaiting her orders, had not changed at all. This was not the case with the cabinets, sculpted by termites, and the silver forks Renata's sisters hadn't taken away, which now sat in the drying rack with tines as greenish and twisted as the relics of a medieval saint. Argenis sat on the bench, following the tracks of the insistent memory of his grandmother sitting on it, pulling stones out of some long-grain rice. Although it worked well enough to keep the refrigerator door in its place, the bench creaked under his weight.

"Get off that, boy," his grandmother shouted. "That thing's got termites."

When the coffee was ready, she served it in two large mugs with boiling milk, placing them on the tray that had once belonged to her masters, and setting the whole thing on an ottoman with a Star of David, which sat between two rocking chairs facing the television. Argenis sat down with the old woman, who was spreading butter on a cracker without taking her eyes from the news, making loud comments about the reports with the same passion and ignorance she used for the twists and revelations of the telenovelas. It doesn't matter, Argenis thought; she has watched history pass her by just as passively as her telenovelas. It had never occurred to her to intervene, to rebel, to poison her oppressors.

As soon as he realized how closely he resembled his grandmother, he was full of contempt for himself. He was so arrogant. In that, he also resembled her. His father, on the other hand, even if he was a hypocrite, had at least tried to do something to change things. What had Consuelo done? Put up with it. Put up with it like Rocky in the first *Rocky*. Put up with it without being KO'd by the fifty years of greasy pans and someone else's dirty panties.

Argenis took advantage of the hypnotic power the television exercised over his grandmother to observe her thoroughly. Her Milky Way-colored skin was plowed with wrinkles as precise and as deep as the marks left in an old folded letter. Her eyes were still beautifully happy, young, curious, and without eyelashes, full of a generosity his Aunt Niurka had inherited. Without removing them from the screen, she took Argenis's now-empty mug from his hand and told him to get the sweets and bring them to San Miguel. He followed her to her room and confirmed his suspicions. At night the house was as empty as the run-down museum of a long-gone middle class, while its strange curator returned to her room off the courtyard, to the same rusty bed frame with a new mattress Consuelo had only recently accepted, reluctantly, from her children.

The servant's room was smaller than Argenis had remembered, and it belonged to an era even more remote and absurd than Trujillo's or Balaguer's. The walls were bare except for a cross Renata had brought back from her trip to the Holy Land. There was no mirror, no hairbrush, no lipstick, no perfume, no curlers. She picked the bell up off an altar full of empty glasses in order to call her saint. She rang one, two, three times, with little ceremony, bringing the sweets to her mouth and chewing them with difficulty. Argenis was anxious to witness the prodigal spirit that had been the protagonist of so many stories.

"Do you smoke?" his grandmother asked. Argenis offered her the open pack of Nacionals and some matches. Consuelo took one out and lit it, but the flame didn't touch the unlit one-peso candle on the altar. She stood up without even looking at the image of the saint and parted the towel that acted as a curtain over the room's only Persian blind.

"I used to pass food through here to your father when he would come to see me in the middle of the night," she told him. "They were hunting him down to kill him. If you could only have seen him. He looked like a skeleton."

It hadn't been Argenis's lot to live in the time of gods and heroes, he had been born too late, but they had existed, and here was the rusty aluminum blind to prove it. He got up ceremoniously and touched the window with his open hand, just as the pilgrims in Higüey touch the glass covering of Our Lady of Altagracia. He felt a strange force pushing inside him, a kind of spiritual nausea. The atmosphere had become strange: it was pulling everything down, pulling him toward his grandmother's cot, with a stench of sugar, or something like it. And with his eyes closed, he felt his father's panic – the desire he'd had back then to change the world, with death nipping at his heels.

The woman had dreamy tits, round as melons and crowned by a Tibetan pendant that fell right down to her cleavage. Her hands were perhaps too delicate for a really good wank. Argenis knew that the more masculine a woman's hands, the better hand jobs she gave. But her mouth was large and fleshy and Argenis imagined her stretching it out to the limit like elastic on panties in order to eagerly swallow his cock, and later opening her legs right there on the desk to offer him her shaved, juicy cunt. She was the director of SOLIDARIA, a Spanish NGO that worked on women's health issues, and Argenis supposed she was probably gay, like the majority of the friends, whether female or "female," of his aunt – or that she was at least "complicated."

Niurka had gotten him the interview. They needed an art teacher to give workshops for victims of gender-based violence. The salary was not exactly generous, but it was enough to pay the rent, electricity, groceries, and phone bills. Besides which, Mar, as the woman was called, had spoken of a vacant space with its own bathroom on the top floor of the building, which he could use as a studio and which was even big enough to house monumental pieces. He walked with her through the facilities into a classroom with individual work tables and an enormous, modern, white marker board. In the center was a round table, perfect for a life model for the anatomical drawing classes. All that was needed was some decent lighting, but only in the afternoon, since the mornings would surely see enough light streaming through the row of east-facing windows.

The classroom was cool and the scent of the centuries-old eucalyptus on the sidewalk wafted through the Persian blinds. Everything was new in the offices; this was the way the motherland eased her guilt complex. They were filled with posters bearing commemorative feminist slogans or announcing some international conference. There were too many ornamental plants for a workplace, and behind every desk was a woman, except for the accountant, an effeminate Frenchman who was the only one to stand when Mar introduced Argenis.

They went up the granite stairs to the third floor which, Argenis guessed from its height and condition, was a recent addition. It was an open studio of about 200 square meters with ceilings three meters high. "In the future, we want to open a space here for art exhibitions and cultural activities, performances, theater, et cetera," Mar said, turning all her Cs into Spanish THs. "In the meantime you can use it for your studio, perhaps for a year and a half or so." The Spanish woman opened the door to the bathroom, which was also new and had a shower. Argenis imagined his host naked under the water.

They went out onto a little south-facing balcony with an iron railing, from which you could see the blue strip of the Caribbean and feel the salt in the wind. On one corner of the balcony was a stack of white plastic chairs. Mar took two down without asking for help and then unwrapped a pack of Marlboro Lights she'd had in her hand the whole time. She tapped the bottom of the box before opening it and after taking one out for herself she offered one to

Argenis, who – like her – was already sitting with his feet up on the railing.

Mar's sandaled feet were white with round, baby-like nails that made you want to put them in your mouth. His, smelly and hairy, were thankfully inside suede moccasins that one of Niurka's lovers had left behind at her place. "You'll have to work with women who have been through it all: physical abuse, rape, psychological abuse. We will give you two weeks of training so that you'll be able to handle any situation that comes up during class, and so that you can prepare your syllabus. Rather than an art class, think of what you're doing as occupational therapy."

Mar's Catalan accent made her even more attractive, and Argenis thought of the acne-filled face of his brother as a teenager in order to avoid an erection. The idea of wrestling with the emotional ups and downs of abused women didn't appeal to him, but after four years without even picking up a paintbrush the prospect of a fixed salary and a workspace did. There, with the ocean breeze and the company of a beautiful woman, he felt content. In many ways, a job where he could show up in shorts and sandals, and through which he could be of some help, was ideal.

Mar got up, threw her cigarette into the street, and put out her hand to seal the deal at the same instant that Argenis's cell phone started to vibrate in his shirt pocket. He took the thing out and asked his new boss for a moment with a gesture of the eyes and hand. It was Loudón, who was expecting him at his workshop to try on the suit. When he finished speaking, Mar had already dropped her hand. She accompanied him to the first floor and said, by way of a farewell, that he should look at the institution's web page in order to familiarize himself with it.

Independencia Avenue was packed with minibuses and *conchos* and they were honking their horns incessantly, as if the unbearable noise might unravel the blocks-long traffic jam. The driver of the *concho* Argenis was traveling in got out to try to make out the cause of the problem in the distance. But the problem was very far away and the driver saw how dozens of others like him were also getting out of their cars to look ahead. They had been stuck there, unmoving, for half an hour under a deluge of curses the passengers were hurling down at the country, the drivers, the government, their own lives.

Argenis got out and stepped onto the sidewalk to walk to the tailor's shop. It was only a few blocks. When he got to the cemetery, those responsible for the traffic jam – some employees of the Electric Company – were up on a service truck's ladder in the middle of the street, repairing a transformer. It was common for the transformers to explode and leave several blocks without electricity. A high-voltage cable had broken and fallen into the street, and a couple of technicians had roped it off. The ones who were up on the ladder were illuminating their work with lights from their hard hats – the last rays of the sun would go down at any moment.

Arzobispo Nouel Street looked dark and desolate, lit only by the lights from a *colmado* fed by an emergency generator. An old woman was assiduously sweeping outside the front of the tailor shop. Argenis thought it might be the mother or aunt of the tailor, but the woman, who had one eye half closed, kept sweeping until she got to the corner, then turned and disappeared. The workshop looked empty. Presumably, when he'd heard the news of the power outage, Loudón had called his clients to tell them not to come. It was dinnertime and one of his assistants was eating a plate of spaghetti with bread; she was sitting in the doorway to take advantage of the light from the *colmado*. It smelled of tomato sauce and cheese. In a nasal voice the woman told him that Orestes was inside.

To make it possible to work, Orestes had placed a number of candles in the four corners of the room. One was on his sewing machine, one hung over the wardrobe where he kept the pieces that were ready to be picked up, one on the bottle of the water dispenser, and the fourth right on the floor. They all surrounded a round rug that looked black by candlelight, but could have been purple or navy blue. Under the light from the water-bottle candle, Loudón was tossing a spoonful of black powder into a plastic jar. "It's charcoal," he told Argenis, dividing the contents into two glasses. Offering him one, he said, "Drink; this absorbs everything that's of no use." When Argenis, confused, brought it to his mouth, he added, "It's good for your stomach."

Orestes Loudón emptied his own in one slow, silent gulp. One drop escaped from between his lips and traced a black line, which could have been red, down to his throat. Argenis, who drank his murky water in sips, felt the hairs on his head, which he had shaved that morning along with his beard, stand up.

The power outage had shut off the fans and Loudón took his shirt off to cool down. When he came over to take back the empty glass, Argenis saw scars on his hands that extended like gloves of wrinkled skin up to his shoulders, as if the man had stuck both his arms into hot lava. His chest was covered by very black curly hair that dipped below his belt and, although he didn't look like a weakling, his shoulder blades stuck out from his back like the mounds of dead roots big trees left in the ground many years after being cut down.

As the tailor took the nearly finished suit from its plastic cover, a cold wind blew through the window, agitating the candle flames and projecting dancing shadows onto the walls. The suit and shirt were white: it was a tropical suit, like the ones diplomatic protocol required for certain receptions, and the ones kids with villas at Casa de Campo used for their parties at the marina. Argenis had never worn a suit like that – in fact, the only time he had worn a suit jacket at all it had been an old one of his brother's, which he wore for Leonel Fernández's presidential inauguration.

It was a one-button jacket with pointy lapels, and the pants were cut straight and narrow. Dazzled by this marvel, Argenis stood in the middle of the circular rug, where he undressed in just as much of a hurry as his father had done twenty years earlier, and kicked his clothes and shoes far away, opening his arms into a cross so that the suit's creator could help him into it. Once Argenis had it on, Loudón moved the candles in front of the wall mirror so that, multiplied by the reflection, they could light his client more intensely. Then he made Argenis turn around and look at himself while he took some pins from a beat-up, apple-shaped pincushion, deftly sticking their ends between his teeth.

Under that primitive light Argenis looked like an apparition, a cut-out silhouette on a black background, the very spirit of elegance. He thought of *The Nobleman with his Hand on his Chest* by El Greco and, like that man, he put his hand on his solar plexus like someone taking an oath.

Loudón asked him to raise his arms again so he could use the pins to mark the spots that needed adjustment: the shoulders, the waist, the hem. The tailor went about his work in silence, allowing his client to remain standing before himself. This really was a work of art, Argenis thought, admiring the exquisite cut, the symmetry of the parts, the fall of the fabric over his limbs, the way in which the white contrasted with his bronze-colored mulatto's skin. For the first time since he had graduated from Chavón he felt he was part of a relevant creative process, that this new Argenis, the one who peered at him from the mirror, was his concept, his work of art, the new man, as Che Guevara used to say – and here he couldn't help but let out a chuckle.

With the laughter and movement, the pin Loudón was putting into the waistband pricked Argenis a little. "This one's the first of many," Loudón said. "You'll see how quickly you'll get to like going around like this." Argenis felt light, capable of anything, capable above all of visiting his father and asking him for money, a job, attention. Dressed this way it was impossible to imagine wasting his talent for drawing on women with black eyes who had no real interest in fine arts. A feeling of disdain for his aunt's world made him lift his chin and he looked at the noble profile that his mother's genes had bestowed on him, the stomach that addiction had smoothed, the height that surpassed that of his father and his brother, the slanted, feline eyes and the long-fingered, expressive hands that his past lovers had so praised.

Something made a noise in the outer room. "The cat, hunting mice," said Loudón, now without pins in his mouth, as he took two steps back to contemplate his work and to smile, showing all his teeth, some of them pearly, and one golden like the morning star.

The door opened behind them and José Alfredo Luna entered. Argenis felt a strange calmness inside and it didn't matter to him if it was a coincidence or if Loudón had set up the meeting. If it had been a mother and daughter, a seamstress would have praised her client: "Look how pretty your daughter is," "She looks like a princess." But these were men, and Loudón remained silent, contenting himself with moving his eyebrows and subtly nodding toward Argenis to show José Alfredo what he had achieved.

Argenis also remained silent as he spun around, with José Alfredo's same smile, with José Alfredo's same almond-shaped eyes, lifting his butt the way his father had once done, too, incarnating for his father an impossible vision of himself, a vision of life and hope, of youth, swollen with blood, claiming its place in the world. And that vision of his fingers on another hand, his lips on another face, suddenly sucked the life from José Alfredo. He felt like a container, useful only for his experiences, like a *señor*, like a fucking old man. He dropped into the white plastic chair by the door like a sack of potatoes. The electricity came back on, to the general rejoicing of the barrio and the noisy tears of José Alfredo. Argenis finally dropped his pose and kneeled in front of his father to wipe away his tears and say, "Papi, you're the man. I'm here, with you. I love you."

Loudón asked him to take off the suit so he could finish it and, giving them each a glass of water, sent them off to sit in the waiting room. An old bachata, "Medicina de Amor," was playing in the *colmado* across the way. The only thing he and his father agreed on was their hatred for bachata. Argenis closed the door onto the street, but it did not prevent the noisy guitar from filtering through the woodwork. His old man had removed the gold-framed glasses he always wore. His eyes had bags underneath, crow's feet, and little cream-colored warts. They looked like the eyes of a gremlin. He appeared tired and defenseless after months of dirty campaigning, intrigue, hustling. Like always, the triumph of his party had cost him tears, blood, and a significant portion of dignity. Age had come upon him and Argenis, seeing his father defeated by biology, couldn't even recall the thirst for vengeance he had felt only a few hours earlier.

"Son, what happened in Cuba – let me explain," he tried to tell Argenis, but Argenis got ahead of him and said, "Don't worry, Dad. Everything's fine." Just like on that distant afternoon when he had guided his father into the tailor shop, he felt compassion, a need to take care of him. His father owed him a suit, a pair of sneakers, a bunch of stuff – but he owed his father his life, a life that in Orestes Loudón's waiting room seemed to him immense and full of pleasures still to be discovered. That impeccable suit had awoken an unknown pride within him; that stitched-together fabric not only made him look distinguished and attractive, but also had restored the world to him in a lustrous splendor. He felt the vigorous thrust of his youth, recognized a richness in his young age that his father and Loudón both envied, and that tender envy made him feel powerful.

Loudón appeared with the suit on a plastic-covered hanger and, when José Alfredo made as if to pull out his wallet, he explained that his son had already paid. The bureaucrat put his wallet back in his jacket pocket and went out onto the street, holding Argenis's hand as if he were a child. José Alfredo's driver brought the black Lexus SUV up to the sidewalk and got out to open the door for them. José Alfredo let his son get in first, then the suit, and then finally climbed in himself. Another bachata, this one by Aventura, ruined the moment's perfection, but as soon as José Alfredo closed the door behind him and both of them were inside the luxurious vehicle Romeo Santos' voice disappeared completely, as if by magic.

Avocado stuffed with crab
Crab legs with garlic and parsley
Shrimp in vinegar
Tuna carpaccio
Grilled squid
Shrimp cocktail
Crab cocktail
Galician-style imported octopus
Half dozen Blue Point oysters
Spanish tortilla

Just reading the appetizer menu of the Don Pepe restaurant made Argenis's throat start to itch. His father had forgotten that he was allergic and ordered one of everything for the table, to share with Pellín and Aquiles, two old buddies who, like José Alfredo, now worked at the National Palace. Argenis said nothing, waiting for the Spanish tortilla and the French wine his father had ordered with the only French he had. He had known Pellín and Aquiles since he was a baby, from the meetings his father had held at their home when he was still married to Etelvina. Back then they had hidden their bony faces behind beards that emulated Fidel's and wore guayabera shirts eaten up by the kind of sweat known only to Caribbean pedestrians. They were broke, jobless, and they fell on the *sancocho* stew Etelvina made for them as if they hadn't eaten in years.

They ate now with that same desperation, and his father – even though he had better manners than they did, thanks to his second wife – slurped his oysters noisily. They talked with their mouths full – about their golden years, their dead comrades, the hard times they'd endured in the mountains, Cuba, as if they had to justify their excessive appetites to Argenis. Pellín nudged José Alfredo with his elbow, since his hand was dirty, and told Argenis, "Your father was a daredevil. His pulse never went up at all, not like these fags." Argenis wondered what fags they were talking about. Was a contingent of fags trying to topple the government? Pellín and Aquiles disgusted him. They were creatures lacking any grace, leeches who survived by attaching themselves to any possibility of notoriety. Their premium linen suits and chubby wrists adorned with heavy Bulova watches added a picturesque touch to the ensemble, something historical and clinical, like Velázquez's dwarves.

When the lobsters thermidor arrived, as monstrous as their consumers, he felt a bit embarrassed and recognized the disapproving looks directed their way by the old-money white guys at neighboring tables. This is the Dominican Revolution, he told himself with a shank of lamb in his mouth. So much blood spilled, just to eat lobster. His father was obsessed with lobsters. One time, when they were on vacation at Tony Catrain's house in Las Terrenas, he had made them stand barefoot on the burning hot sand of the beach at midday. Ernesto had spit out a piece of lobster. Since Argenis was allergic he didn't have to eat it, but his father had punished the two of them, just as he and his comrades had been punished when they were all in prison during the first few years of Balaguer's dictatorship.

José Alfredo would pardon anything, except their turning their noses up at their food. Ernesto had a good appetite, but he hated shellfish. José Alfredo had made him pick up the lobster he'd thrown on the floor and swallow it. When Argenis saw his brother chew that blob with grains of sand on it, his eyes filled with tears.

"Do you know what your dad ate in jail?" José Alfredo asked them. "Do you know what *chow* is?" Tony Catrain had sent Charlie to his room to save him from the scene and tried unsuccessfully to intercede on behalf of the children: "José Alfredo, leave them alone, they're kids."

"*Chow*, you ingrates," José Alfredo continued, "was a concoction made of leftovers, ground-up rice, chicken claws, the prison guards' phlegm and snot, really delicious. And they made your daddy drink it down, and if he complained he had to swallow an entire potful, along with a couple of kicks to the balls." Ernesto started gagging. "Swallow it, damn it," José Alfredo ordered. Tony Catrain watched them from the patio, both hands on his waist. Ernesto tried to swallow twice, and the third time everything he had ingested since breakfast came out of his mouth. In the vomit, you could recognize bits of scrambled egg and Choco Rica. The horrible leather sandals with thin socks that José Alfredo used for the beach disgusted Argenis even more than his brother's vomit on the sand. He raised his head, and looking his father in the eyes, said, "I'm going to tell Mami."

Etelvina never went away with them during Holy Week. She stayed in the capital, taking a break from the boys, from José Alfredo, from school. Argenis knew his father would never have dared to do this in front of her, and he knew who won the shouting matches that back then his parents had almost every night. Transformed by the words of his youngest son, José Alfredo went to Ernesto with a concerned expression and asked, "Are you OK?" It was obvious he wasn't. He picked up Ernesto's little ten-year-old body and laid it on the sofa in the living room, made him an anise tea, and had Argenis fan him with a folder. Tony Catrain didn't invite them to Las Terrenas ever again.

His father told the anecdote and his friends guffawed loudly. Argenis laughed too. Ernesto was a son of a bitch who no longer roused any sympathy in him. The noise bothered the other customers – their bursts of laughter were even more annoying to the Dominican petit bourgeoisie than the Molotovs they'd thrown in the Autonomous University in 1970. In the midst of the laughter, a grain of rice from Pellín's mouth landed on Argenis's plate. Although he still had his shank of lamb, Argenis considered the food finished.

The memory of his grandmother cleaning the rice wormed its way into his body. It wasn't a two-dimensional image – she was there with him. Consuelo was smiling impishly, showing her missing tooth, and, holding a tiny stone she had just extracted between her fingers, she said, "In this world, there are those who clean it, and those who eat it." Was she talking about the rice, or the world? Argenis had no idea. His father's friends were grinning vacantly at him like marionettes as they licked the tips of fingers thick as sausages. He felt nauseous and excused himself to go to the bathroom, where he urinated and threw some water on his face, his neck, his wrists. He looked into the mirror and felt better. As he pushed down on the soap dispenser he thought of Susana. How she would marvel over his father's table, over that liquid soap that never stopped flowing.

When he came out of the bathroom, he saw José Alfredo enjoying a crème brûlée, and at the next table a waiter was seating a pair of attractive forty-somethings. The man wore his hair gelled back, a polo shirt and khaki shorts; the woman a strapless linen tube dress. It was Giorgio Menicucci and his wife, Linda Goldman. Three years ago they had given Argenis a scholarship on the north coast. He didn't have to do anything except paint and pay attention to the Cuban curator they had brought over. Argenis didn't keep his side of the bargain. He had had a nervous breakdown, made himself ridiculous. When they kicked him out he came back to the capital in such bad condition that his father had him committed to the mental health ward of the UCE that same day. He didn't want them to see him. He wanted the earth to swallow him up.

Giorgio got up from his chair, took two strides, and put his hand on José Alfredo's shoulder, who greeted him with an affection Argenis knew was feigned. He felt embarrassed by the airs his father gave himself whenever rich white people said a word to him. Then Giorgio looked at Argenis and, without greeting Pellín or Aquiles, opened his arms as if waiting for a hug. It would have been very awkward not to return the gesture. "Can I borrow the maestro for a few minutes?" he asked José Alfredo, referring to Argenis with a mock nineteenth-century courtesy which José Alfredo, passing a dirty napkin from one hand to the other, also failed to detect.

Maestro. He had called him maestro. He could only be called that as a joke or with the intention to hurt. He hadn't painted a thing in years. Nevertheless, Giorgio was looking at him with something more akin to admiration than pity. It was strange; Argenis didn't know what to attribute it to. Giorgio's gestures were careful and respectful toward him, and his wife's eyes sparkled when she greeted him. They asked where he had been and he invented some experimental performance art he'd done in Havana: "Some research into the limits of the socialist body," he said. He was talking like Susana, and they loved it.

Linda took his hand and the gesture surprised him. She looked at him with eyes that didn't seem to lie and said, "Argenis, it's so good to see you well." They had broken the ice and all of them were feeling more relaxed. Giorgio ordered a glass for the gentleman and they served him a delicious ice-cold prosecco. They had started to build a conservation laboratory for the reefs on the north coast, and the art gallery was doing well. "That's what we wanted to talk to you about," Linda said, looking at her husband as if she were about to announce a pregnancy. "We have a collector who's very interested in your work."

During the Sosúa grant, he had painted a number of canvases with motifs from his mental illness, phantasmal buccaneers who were flaying cows. As he painted them he could smell the blood of those animals in the red acrylic. It was an intense trip that he ended up believing in. The day they threw him out, he had sworn that Giorgio was the reincarnation of one of those buccaneers, either that or a demon. Argenis had gotten violent. He didn't even like to remember it. It shamed him. He had imagined that those paintings weren't worth a cent and that Giorgio and Linda had thrown them in the trash, just like him.

It hadn't been like that. Linda had always preferred painting to conceptual art. "I saved them so I could give them to you when you were better," she said, and Argenis appreciated the gesture, forgiving her the condescension common to all gringos. They were talking about a collector, about money. They were talking about a solo exhibition at the gallery, a studio, new work, possible exhibitions in Europe and, after ordering another bottle of prosecco, they asked if he could please get them an audience with the president. They wanted to talk to him about the laboratory, ask for funding, money to fulfill their capricious environmental dreams.

Argenis understood the power being a satellite of his father's would confer upon him. He weighed up what was in play. His face did not darken. On the contrary, he smiled with the same hypocrisy as Aquiles and Pellín. "You can count on it," he told them. Now that he had something the Menicuccis wanted, he saw them in a very different light. No longer were they the epitome of good taste and cool. They were just another couple of hustlers. He got up to go in order to make himself more important, but not before leaving them a little piece of paper with the number of the cheap cell phone Niurka had loaned him.

A knife traces a slit from the throat to the anus of the cow. They are skinning it. That black hand belongs to a man dressed in a bloodstained linen tunic. He is carrying a kind of arquebus on his shoulder and has a purple rag tied around his head. In his right hand, which coincides with the upper-right corner of the painting, he is holding up a leg, a leg from a reality that doesn't exist in any other part of the painting. You could count the hairs surrounding the hoof, see the dirt stuck to the hoof. You could feel the animal's past vitality in that leg. In the lower-left corner another man is kneeling, a white man. With both hands clinging to one side of the gash that has divided the cow's skin, he is pulling outwards. There is blood everywhere. The grass has turned red, purple, black. The white man has a knife in his mouth. Where his eyes should be there are a couple of gray smudges made with a spatula, as if his features had been liquefied – the way you sometimes see the features of two people mixed together in dreams. In some areas the paint has been applied with too much water and it drips. Inside the gash there are no guts, no flesh, no bones. What peeks out is a blue, the iridescent blue of a pool. It's as if a David Hockney were living inside a Francis Bacon cow. The buccaneers are peering into that portal. They are going to extract a Hockney from the cow.

Argenis would never have been able to paint that now. He remembered creating the piece, but he couldn't recall all the details. Where had he gotten such bravery? Those thick brushstrokes on the muscled arms of the buccaneers? Those accidental-seeming stains that made distant features of the tropical landscape jump out of the canvas? The little drops of Vermeer-like light he had used to bring the hands to life? What he did remember were the names of those men, names his psychosis had told him. Roque, Ngome – buccaneers who made their living from wild cattle. They sold their hides to smugglers. He didn't know if he had invented them to feed his paintings or if he had painted them in order to be able to deal with their insistent and inopportune presence.

"We could ask ten thousand dollars for this one," Linda Goldman said, standing in front of the work. She was wearing sweaty workout clothing from a Zumba session at the gym and sucking water from a little pink plastic water bottle. They were in the gallery's basement, an art storage space with polished cement floors and climate control. Giorgio Menicucci had pulled the piece off the shelf and was holding it up by one corner. He was looking at it with the very same face his father used to admire lobsters. The price was not bad for an emerging artist.

These paintings have had a better time of it than I have, here in this air-conditioned gallery, admired and taken care of, Argenis thought as they went back up the stairs to the first floor, where the exhibit space was located. Pieces of skateboards, used tires, broken trucks, and bits of boards rested on little white shelves, the ready-mades of a Puerto Rican artist's first solo exhibition in the DR. On the back wall a video was being projected: a skateboarder was stitching up a wound in his own knee. The curved needle looked like a fishhook and the skin appeared dark-green from the blow. The guy pushed the needle in without a fuss.

Behind an opaque glass wall was the office. They sat in there and Giorgio pulled a bottle of Albariño out of a mini-fridge. Argenis made a mental inventory of the furniture, the Swedish desks, the Philippe Starck lamps, the shelves full of Phaidon and Taschen volumes, art magazines and critical theory organized by the color of their spines. Not a speck of dust sullied the white walls. He imagined a performance art piece with the woman who cleaned the gallery, the one who was really responsible for that immaculate space.

"That seems fine," Argenis told Linda, regarding the price, "but I'll need an advance." She looked surprised and shot a glance at her husband so quick it just about broke her neck.

"How much do you need?" asked Giorgio.

Argenis made a rough calculation. There were six pieces and they would keep 50 percent. Thirty thousand and thirty thousand. "I need eight thousand dollars," he asked, worrying that he'd gone too far. Linda breathed a sigh of relief and opened the desk drawer to remove a checkbook. Argenis regretted having asked for so little, although he'd never before seen such a sum next to his name.

He saw himself breaking down Rambo's door, convincing him to get him a thousand dollars of H. He'd take that heroin wisely, over a few months. He'd rent an apartment in front of the Mirador where he could shoot up, and he'd buy a stereo. Maybe he'd paint. Maybe he'd buy a TV and a DVD player. A computer. He imagined himself putting the needle in while lying on the sofa he'd buy too, beatified by the light of the sunset, his father's lobsters thermidor crawling toward him from all over.

When Susana and he had been dreaming about the life the 500 dollars Bengoa got from José Alfredo was going to buy them, she told him they'd eat lobster every day. He was allergic, Argenis reminded her, and she kissed him on the mouth as if her kisses were antihistamine. He concentrated on looking at Linda's ass to avoid thinking of Susana and Bengoa fucking on the sofa. Giorgio poured three glasses of the Albariño and toasted the beginning of a new stage in Argenis's life. Argenis drank it in one gulp, pulled the check from his pocket, and kissed both Linda and Giorgio. He pushed open the door of the gallery with his back, looking at the check he held in both hands, and before leaving, he lied to them: "Papi's on it already." He hadn't spoken to his father, nor was he going to. He wasn't going to Rambo's, either.

The gallery was located in the new downtown area, on a Lincoln Avenue recently built up with beige or sand-colored towers and huge liquor stores with Spanglish names. You could breathe in the economic well-being, except for a brigade of Haitians in rags who were drilling a huge hole into the sidewalk cement. They belonged to another century, to a sepia-toned world of mud and lamentations.

An Apollo Taxi stopped and Argenis asked the driver to take him to a Banco Popular. He wanted to cash his check as soon as possible, feel the gasoline smell of those bills. They headed toward 27 Febrero Avenue and, despite all of Argenis's warnings, the driver decided to take it. It was two p.m. and one giant traffic jam ran up and down it for kilometers, for its entire length. The faces of the pedestrians waiting on the sidewalks for *conchos* and buses wore an endemic sadness, a mixture of resentment and acceptance, of hate dressed up as debauchery. Desperation dressed in a Burger King uniform was holding up prepaid cell phones with monstrous Chinese porcelain fingernails. Decades of shit, of systematic looting, of public schools that were just farms for containment, had sculpted that dizzying, endless wave of eyes. Who could defend them, thought Argenis, now that the elected officials had turned into ruminants? Would it be up to him? To his frivolous friends? "There's no way to fix this," he said aloud, and the driver, who thought he was talking about the traffic, said, "Don't worry, buddy. Up ahead this shit'll thin out."

He chose the green suitcase for its color. He wanted to believe that just as the green balanced the red, this suitcase would bring him better luck, bring him a destiny that was positively complementary to the strange and desperate one his mother's red suitcase had provided in Cuba. It was a Samsonite bag, a bit expensive, made of cloth, modern and hard. Unlike the red one, it would have survived the adventure with Vantroi, full of costumes and scenery.

The employee who sold it to him, a Colombian with transparent braces on his teeth, told him that the suitcase was "cool," pressing his lips together in pleasure as he opened it like the skirt of a lover to show off the inside. Argenis imagined that anyone seeing it would do the same, and made his decision. Now that he was walking with it, empty, along El Conde Street he felt how cool it was, what its compact design added to him, as he very carefully made a mental list of the products he'd fill it with. The space was limited and everything should have a certain importance and significance. Like in a painting. He wanted to bring art supplies and quality wines, clothing to give away, cheeses, chewing gum and chocolates, books and magazines, things he should buy on the other side of the city, in the Supermercado Nacional or Plaza Central.

The cell phone Niurka had loaned him rang and he pulled it out of his pocket, saw it was his father. José Alfredo had threatened to call him and talk about a few things. Argenis felt tired just imagining those things. Being introduced to the president, a possible appointment. He ignored the call and stopped on the corner of Hostos Street to hail a taxi. Just then a cloud emptied itself like a bucket as the sun hid away. He ran with the other pedestrians to take shelter under the decrepit eaves of an art deco building, and from there he glanced over at the Cafetería El Conde a block away, where he had spent all those afternoons with the old painters when he was studying at Fine Arts. Back then he liked the place because it was the closest thing to Van Gogh's *Café Terrace at Night* and, now that the rain had stopped and the water was making the cobblestones reflect the light from the recently lit streetlamps, he was filled with a sentimentality that made him think of all the troubles poor Vincent had endured.

On the way to the café the green wheels of his suitcase raised little droplets from the ground. From far away, just as he used to, he made out the customers sitting on the patio, so that he could head straight to the painters' table and avoid the poets, practically all of whom were nineteenth-century pseudo-intellectuals with halitosis. The painters' table, next to one of the entrances, was empty and they had replaced the old hexagonal metal ashtray with the Montecarlo logo with a cheap, round, glass one. The star waiter, Abreu, flitted between the other tables. In spite of his white hair, he hadn't acquired even one new wrinkle. Abreu recognized him as soon as he saw him and said, "Good evening, sir. Céspedes is inside."

José Céspedes was the only survivor of that roundtable. The other members had died unceremoniously, their work remembered only in brief, pictureless columns that the editors of the culture pages had begrudgingly written. He was sitting at a square two-top near the bathroom and the ceiling fan inside the cafeteria, wearing a pair of green Ray-Ban sunglasses that were too large for a face that had lost all its flesh. Céspedes was a skull, a skull with a five o'clock shadow and warts so big they reminded Argenis of tufts of cotton escaping through tears in a stuffed animal. He was bald, and his ears hung down as huge as steaks and the rotten cashew of a nose was covered with blackheads big as the points of pencils. Someone had set two paintings for sale on the two chairs next to him. On both of them, tremulous lines attempted to evoke the façade of the cathedral. It wasn't the attempt of a child; it was the achievement of someone trying to paint from memory or from a dream, with lines over whose flow vision no longer had any control. Céspedes had gone blind.

Argenis leaned in to the painter and whispered, "Maestro, it's me, Argenis Luna." Céspedes smiled and extended a hand to touch his face. His hand smelled like piss, but Argenis allowed him to touch his cheek, happy to make the old man smile. That sack of bones had been the cause of magical afternoons. He had recounted a world history of painting for Argenis as if it were a fairy tale, had bought him beer, wine, and cigarettes, had blessed him, had recognized the talent within him. Now penniless, with a dirty, stinking olive-green shirt over which no perfumed scarf now waved, Céspedes still inspired great benevolence and admiration in Argenis. He ordered a large Presidente and a pack of Nacionals. He praised the paintings and asked their prices. Céspedes drily said they had already been sold. Sensing he had offended him, Argenis changed the subject. They spoke of dead friends, of Ovando, Piñal, the girls that – according to him – were still falling for him, the women who said he looked like he was forty. Argenis forced a laugh.

Abreu came back with ice-cold beer and two glasses. Céspedes searched for his lighter with an open hand on his shirt pocket. Argenis noticed the clean nails that some-one had apparently cut for him. The painter lit the cig-arette and the nicotine took two or three years off him. Argenis couldn't stop looking at the two paintings with their floating cathedrals, the solidity of those animals, trains, and shoes that the clouds drew in the sky and which lasted as long as the air took to unmake them. Céspedes's paintings, although figurative, had always had a light consistency: he translated the excessive impact of the tropical light on the city into white areas, spaces with no paint. There, where the sun hit the hardest, was where the void was found. Santo Domingo, his favorite subject, was a luminous, crystalline place in his paintings. Maybe he's always been blind, thought Argenis. As the old man coughed into a handkerchief, he recalled an atypi-cal green series, in which Céspedes had depicted himself talking with internationally known painters like José Luis Cuevas, Wifredo Lam, Warhol. And there was a pink series in which he painted himself with diva songstresses, but especially Cher – Céspedes was obsessed with Cher. He couldn't stop coughing, and Argenis asked for some water for his friend. When Abreu brought the water, Céspedes stood up, still coughing, and accidentally knocked it to the ground by accident. He made a move to help pick it up and Argenis could see the disgusting contents of the handkerchief.

The cough forced the old man to sit down again, and Argenis got up to pay their check. At the cash register, Abreu asked him to walk the painter home. He did it every day, but it wasn't yet closing time.

"Did you really sell the paintings?" Argenis asked.

"No, *mijo*, they've been there for weeks," the waiter confessed. Argenis went back to the table, gathered up the maestro's little cathedrals, and put them into the green suitcase, then helped him to his feet with the funny "upa, upa" sounds one makes to a baby. They started on their way to the old man's studio, an enormous one on El Conde Street that Argenis had always envied.

The stores were beginning to shut their noisy metal doors, and the street filled with employees in uniforms of different colors. The rain had stopped and a pleasant breeze was blowing. Céspedes walked in silence, dragging his worn Florsheims; Argenis didn't want to break the silence with banalities. He knew the way, populated as always with male prostitutes in tight jeans looking for business with Europeans; Goth chicks with piercings all over; and boiled corn on the cob vendors who were pedaling their way back to Los Mina.

They came to the building, a solid, Trujillo-era construction which had once been luxury offices but now housed Haitians, prostitutes, and Céspedes. Céspedes had bought the apartment in the seventies when a gallery owner who had managed to hang his paintings in the houses of the Balaguerist petit bourgeoisie had paid him in dollars. In this open space, which in the fifties had housed desks, granite floors, and wide windows, Céspedes had painted almost his entire oeuvre. When they opened the door a stench of shit and rot hit them, turning Argenis's stomach. Though it wasn't necessary, the old man told him where to find the light switch. There was trash everywhere – cans of beans, bottles full of cigarette butts, egg cartons. I should have drunk more before coming, thought Argenis. Céspedes pulled him by his shirtsleeve to the far end of the studio. There the air was clearer and the music from a *colmado* rose from the street. There were several enormous pieces leaning against a wall. The old man felt his way to them with both hands and pushed them to the floor in order to show Argenis what was behind. They were creatures of his new darkness: the darkness inside him had replaced the solar white. Shadows of satyrs, claws, and hens, amorphous blobs, and finally, a depiction of Saturn devouring his son that Céspedes had extracted like a tumor from the back of his memory. Close up, the painting was abstract, but from far away you could recognize the watery forms of Goya's masterwork.

"Saturn ate his children so they wouldn't destroy him," the old man said, raising his voice above the dembow from the *colmado*. "Saturn was a son of a bitch, like Balaguer." Between each sentence he sucked so hard on his cigarette that a centimeter of paper burned off with each drag. "Jupiter's mom hid him on an island and when he came of age, he castrated his father," he continued. "His virility gone, Saturn turned into a mortal and was crowned a king on Earth. His reign is known as the Golden Age." His tone was sarcastic. "There were no thieves, no murderers, and wealth was divided up equally." The old man gave the finger to heaven and shouted, "Saturn, son of a fucking bitch!"

Niurka's little cell phone started ringing again. It was his father. He'd rather smell Céspedes's shit than get hit with José Alfredo's offers of progression. He thought of Niurka's breast, of the job with Mar. He thought of the buccaneers he had painted in Sosúa on scholarship. He would have liked to show them to his teacher. He went over to the old man and grabbed his wrist, saying, "Maestro, I want to show you one of my works." Céspedes was silent. Argenis closed his eyes to see it better, and began to tell him:

"Two men are skinning an animal. They are buccaneers in linen shirts stained with blood. The stains are ocher because the blood is dry, but the blood on the grass at their feet hasn't yet dried. A shifting mass of ochers and reds is accumulating on top of the sap-green of the grass; in that puddle, the paint has been applied directly from the tube onto the canvas. A few blades of grass are very precise, like scientific illustrations, and that precision in the midst of all the imprecision mimics the way vision moves in and out of focus. The blood on the grass is the blood from the cow they are opening up. On the right of the painting, a black man is cutting it open, a purple rag around his head and a period weapon on his shoulder. A musket? No, it's an arquebus. He is a man with powerful muscles. The muscles have a Goyaesque appearance – the brushwork is thick and appears careless, but that carelessness is the brute force unleashed by the painter's hand. The muscles convey that force. On the other side of the cow is a boy with much lighter skin, long hair, and a felt hat. He is grabbing one edge of the gash his friend has created and pulling to free the skin. He has a knife between his teeth. The teeth, small and ashy, peek around the silver blade. The light glints annoyingly off the blade, and his lips brush against it dangerously. Both of their hands are made of thick points of light, like the ornaments on a chair in a Vermeer. The cow's head, applied with a spatula, like the features of the men, hangs to one side. The black man is holding up a hoof, which I put everything into. Caravaggio would gladly have signed that hoof. The hairs around it, Maestro, what a pleasure they are! Here and there the paint runs, because

I spilled the melted ice from my drink on the canvas – I was painting with it laid out on the floor and I took advantage of the accident. From the hole the men are opening in the cow a vision appears. Water – clear, shallow water, like in Boca Chica. The buccaneers are looking into the depths of the water, as if waiting for something."

Céspedes took off his Ray-Ban sunglasses and Argenis could see his blue-green eyes, like balls of marble. He was crying. Like a bird exposing its wet wings to the sun, he opened his arms wide, the way he did to move about. He went to a metal filing cabinet, all its drawers open and full of brushes. He caressed their tips, pulled a few out and put them back again. Then he crossed to a work table covered in dirty rags, dried-up paint tubes, and electricity bills. When he touched its surface, several used plastic cups fell to the ground. He finally reached a wooden Cohiba cigar box on one corner, opened it, and took out a brush. It was an angled brush with honey-colored bristles. The old man ran his fingers over the mahogany-wood handle, stroked his chin with the bristles, and told Argenis, "I bought this brush in Italy in 1976, on my only trip to Europe, and I swore I'd give it to my heir whenever I found him. It's for you, my dear Argenis."

Now a bolero by Alberto Beltrán was drifting up from the *colmado*. That overblown, nasal sentimentalism was both heroic and virile, and Argenis knew he'd think of it every time he used that gift. The old man asked him to help him lie down, clutching his pupil's arm and emitting small grunts until they reached the bed with the wicker headboard. Argenis removed his shoes, helped him get his legs up, and took his shirt off with difficulty. As he was doing this, Céspedes asked, sleepily, "Did you ever find the woman with the sweet cunt?" Argenis didn't answer, just covered him with a Mexican blanket that had once been orange. The old man snored into his pillow immediately, and his snores attracted a wrinkled gecko to the nightstand from where it would translucently watch over its twin brother's repose.

Real light. Not the light projected by pointless human moons. Not the light that attracts moths. Sunlight, severe, impossible to look at directly with open, unprotected eyes. It descended anciently onto everything, without the mercy of clouds. It warmed the earth, attracted the hunger of plants, sliced into the corners of buildings with shadows, turned material into silhouettes, like a scalpel. That morning was made of light, the hot air coming through the window of his Aunt Niurka's car was made of light. Argenis put his hand out to feel the heat and the breeze, relaxed his wrist so the air would push against his hand, deform it, dance with it.

In the background, in an emerald-colored sea, tiny fishermen were tossing out their nets, surrounded by the golden sparks that a mysterious spirit was showering over the water, their bodies reflecting the blessing. That excess was grounds for complaint, for curses, for fatigue. Harvester of blisters, heart attacks, rot. It dried up rivers, burned down forests, that indomitable angel of destruction. In some places the light was so great that the asphalt turned white, like in Céspedes' paintings. The light softened the grays, turned the cars in the distance into liquid vibrations. He wanted to paint that light, to make it obey him.

Beside him, Niurka was looking for something on the radio, but the reception was bad and you could only make out bits of words. The car speakers were groaning like a UFO about to land in an episode of *The X-Files*. His aunt put her hand between her seat and the emergency break, took out a manila envelope, and passed it to him. The envelope had his name on it and was sealed. Argenis used his teeth to open it and inside he found a negative. It was a 6x6 negative from a Rolleiflex. "Tony Catrain left it for you. Charlie told him you were back in the country," said Niurka. "That's José Alfredo at a demonstration at the Autonomous University in 1969."

Holding the negative between the sun and his eye, he could make out his father. The then-athletic mulatto looked white and the reflection of the sun off the asphalt was black. It took him a few moments to identify the objects surrounding him: they were car tires on fire. The smoke coming out of the burnt tires was the same transparent white. It was an extraterrestrial landscape, like the one Neil Armstrong had marked with his boots that same year. In that strange land, as far away as the moon, José Alfredo was fighting against the class structure, against the Balaguer dictatorship, against the hired thugs who were murdering his friends. His arm was outstretched, hurling a Molotov cocktail toward a police force that did not appear in the photo. He exuded the strength and agility of a Muhammad Ali, and the tight pants and tense biceps could have passed for those of Johnny Ventura. José Alfredo was not a student; he was a leader in the Dominican Popular Movement who had only gotten as far as eighth grade. Back then he was a kind of living god. He had trained in Cuba, he knew Che and was friends with Caamaño, he had recruited hundreds of young people for the constitutionalist side during the war of 1965. Aged fourteen, he had gotten the scar that crossed his forehead from a machete, during a strike, completing the legend.

He returned the negative to its place, the reception suddenly improved, and they heard the pastor on an evangelical station requesting donations for a brother. Argenis felt serene and happy thanks to the dollars in his wallet and the things that filled his suitcase and backpack: new clothes, food, presents. The cell phone Niurka had loaned him rang once more. It was his mother. He listened to her for a few minutes. The more obsolete her advice, the more Argenis loved her. She was happy for him, happy he had sold some pieces, but she didn't understand why he had rejected his father's offer. It was a good opportunity – cultural attaché in a Dominican embassy in Europe.

When he'd hung up he turned off the device and stuck it into Niurka's pocket. Since he still had time they stopped by a coconut vendor. The man poured the water from the coconuts into two Styrofoam cups with ice and, after cutting the flesh free, he passed them the open shells to eat from. They went down to the rocky shore and found a couple of stones to sit on. The white coconut flesh reminded him of Céspedes's paintings again, the light everywhere.

"Why are you going back to Cuba?" Niurka asked, and he told her that he had left something undone. She stood up and ceremoniously opened her arms to the sea, then put her hands on Argenis's head without saying a word, just as his grandmother Consuelo had done so many times. He didn't know what to do, so he fixed his gaze on an enormous anthill. Life bubbled from that hole, flowing like blood, in and out. Some ants were carrying immense pieces of coconut, like slaves; some were scaling the hills of even bigger pieces.

When they got to the airport Niurka gave him two kisses, Spanish-style, something she did outside Spain only when she was drunk, and wished him good luck. He could feel his new suit, the suit his father's tailor had made him, attracting approving looks. He felt healthy and clean, as if an invisible detergent had shaken up his insides. As he checked in at the Cuban Airlines ticket counter, the polyester uniforms of the employees and the seventies design of their lapel pins greeted him like an anachronistic cosmogony. He felt slightly apprehensive and thought about the ants with their immense loads. He wasn't shedding his past – he was confronting it. He was going to look for Susana.

In the security line, some baseball players were cracking crude jokes and telling stories about the night before. Those enormous mulattos had escaped from poverty thanks to their ability to throw balls at ninety miles an hour. He remembered the negative. How many miles per hour had that Molotov been traveling? As he put his navy-blue suede moccasins into the tray, a lump rose in his throat. The love his old man felt for him came to him unblemished, like the homemade bomb at the feet of the police. He looked down at his bare feet, at his flat feet for which the army would have rejected him, a pair of feet that ought to last his whole life and that walked because he ordered them: walk.

With profound thanks to all the friends and relatives who in one way or another supported the writing of this book: Raúl Recio, Miguel Peña, Miguelín de Mena, Bernardo Vega, Abilio Estévez, Viriato Piantini, Lorgia García Peña, Luis Amed Irizarry, Rubén Millán, Gonzalo Frómeta, Sebastián González, Daniel González, and Noelia Quintero Herencia.

Dear readers,

As well as relying on bookshop sales, And Other Stories relies on subscriptions from people like you for many of our books, whose stories other publishers often consider too risky to take on.

Our subscribers don't just make the books physically happen. They also help us approach booksellers, because we can demonstrate that our books already have readers and fans. And they give us the security to publish in line with our values, which are collaborative, imaginative and 'shamelessly literary'.

All of our subscribers:

- receive a first-edition copy of each of the books they subscribe to
- are thanked by name at the end of our subscriber-supported books
- receive little extras from us by way of thank you, for example: postcards created by our authors

BECOME A SUBSCRIBER,
OR GIVE A SUBSCRIPTION TO A FRIEND

Visit andotherstories.org/subscriptions to help make our books happen. You can subscribe to books we're in the process of making. To purchase books we have already published, we urge you to support your local or favourite bookshop and order directly from them – the often unsung heroes of publishing.

OTHER WAYS TO GET INVOLVED

If you'd like to know about upcoming events and reading groups (our foreign-language reading groups help us choose books to publish, for example) you can:

- join our mailing list at: andotherstories.org
- follow us on Twitter: @andothertweets
- join us on Facebook: facebook.com/AndOtherStoriesBooks
- admire our books on Instagram: @andotherpics
- follow our blog: andotherstories.org/ampersand

CURRENT & UPCOMING BOOKS

01 Juan Pablo Villalobos, *Down the Rabbit Hole,* trans. Rosalind Harvey

02 Clemens Meyer, *All the Lights,* trans. Katy Derbyshire

03 Deborah Levy, *Swimming Home*

04 Iosi Havilio, *Open Door,* trans. Beth Fowler

05 Oleg Zaionchkovsky, *Happiness is Possible,* trans. Andrew Bromfield

06 Carlos Gamero, *The Islands,* trans. Ian Barnett

07 Christoph Simon, *Zbinden's Progress,* trans. Donal McLaughlin

08 Helen DeWitt, *Lightning Rods*

09 Deborah Levy, *Black Vodka: ten stories*

10 Oleg Pavlov, *Captain of the Steppe,* trans. Ian Appleby

11 Rodrigo de Souza Leão, *All Dogs are Blue,* trans. Zoë Perry and Stefan Tobler

12 Juan Pablo Villalobos, *Quesadillas,* trans. Rosalind Harvey

13 Iosi Havilio, *Paradises,* trans. Beth Fowler

14 Ivan Vladislavić, *Double Negative*

15 Benjamin Lytal, *A Map of Tulsa*

16 Ivan Vladislavić, *The Restless Supermarket*

17 Elvira Dones, *Sworn Virgin,* trans. Clarissa Botsford

18 Oleg Pavlov, *The Matiushin Case,* trans. Andrew Bromfield

19 Paulo Scott, *Nowhere People,* trans. Daniel Hahn

20 Deborah Levy, *An Amorous Discourse in the Suburbs of Hell*

21 Juan Tomás Ávila Laurel, *By Night the Mountain Burns,* trans. Jethro Soutar

22 SJ Naudé, *The Alphabet of Birds,* trans. the author

23 Niyati Keni, *Esperanza Street*

24 Yuri Herrera, *Signs Preceding the End of the World,* trans. Lisa Dillman

25 Carlos Gamero, *The Adventure of the Busts of Eva Perón,* trans. Ian Barnett

26 Anne Cuneo, *Tregian's Ground,* trans. Roland Glasser and Louise Rogers Lalaurie

27 Angela Readman, *Don't Try This at Home*

28 Ivan Vladislavić, *101 Detectives*

29 Oleg Pavlov, *Requiem for a Soldier,* trans. Anna Gunin

30 Haroldo Conti, *Southeaster,* trans. Jon Lindsay Miles

31 Ivan Vladislavić, *The Folly*

32 Susana Moreira Marques, *Now and at the Hour of Our Death,* trans. Julia Sanches

33 Lina Wolff, *Bret Easton Ellis and the Other Dogs,* trans. Frank Perry

34 Anakana Schofield, *Martin John*

35 Joanna Walsh, *Vertigo*

36 Wolfgang Bauer, *Crossing the Sea,* trans. Sarah Pybus with photographs by Stanislav Krupař

37 Various, *Lunatics, Lovers and Poets: Twelve Stories after Cervantes and Shakespeare*

38 Yuri Herrera, *The Transmigration of Bodies,* trans. Lisa Dillman

39 César Aira, *The Seamstress and the Wind,* trans. Rosalie Knecht

40 Juan Pablo Villalobos, *I'll Sell You a Dog,* trans. Rosalind Harvey

41 Enrique Vila-Matas, *Vampire in Love,* trans. Margaret Jull Costa

42 Emmanuelle Pagano, *Trysting,* trans. Jennifer Higgins and Sophie Lewis

43 Arno Geiger, *The Old King in His Exile,* trans. Stefan Tobler

44 Michelle Tea, *Black Wave*

45 César Aira, *The Little Buddhist Monk,* trans. Nick Caistor

46 César Aira, *The Proof,* trans. Nick Caistor

47 Patty Yumi Cottrell, *Sorry to Disrupt the Peace*

48 Yuri Herrera, *Kingdom Cons,* trans. Lisa Dillman

49 Fleur Jaeggy, *I am the Brother of XX,* trans. Gini Alhadeff

50 Iosi Havilio, *Petite Fleur,* trans. Lorna Scott Fox

51 Juan Tomás Ávila Laurel, *The Gurugu Pledge,* trans. Jethro Soutar

52 Joanna Walsh, *Worlds from the Word's End*

53 Nicola Pugliese, *Malacqua,* trans. Shaun Whiteside

54 César Aira, *The Lime Tree,* trans. Chris Andrews

55 Ann Quin, *The Unmapped Country*

56 Fleur Jaeggy, *Sweet Days of Discipline,* trans. Tim Parks

57 Alicia Kopf, *Brother in Ice,* trans. Mara Faye Lethem

58 Christine Schutt, *Pure Hollywood*

59 Cristina Rivera Garza, *The Iliac Crest,* trans. Sarah Booker

60 Norah Lange, *People in the Room,* trans. Charlotte Whittle

61 Kathy Page, *Dear Evelyn*

62 Alia Trabucco Zerán, *The Remainder,* trans. Sophie Hughes

63 Amy Arnold, *Slip of a Fish*

64 Rita Indiana, *Tentacle,* trans. Achy Obejas

65 Angela Readman, *Something Like Breathing*

66 Gerald Murnane, *Border Districts*

67 Gerald Murnane, *Tamarisk Row*

68 César Aira, *Birthday,* trans. Chris Andrews

69 Ann Quin, *Berg*

70 Fleur Jaeggy, *Proleterka,* trans. Alastair McEwen

71 Olivia Rosenthal, *To Leave with the Reindeer,* trans. Sophie Lewis

72 Lina Wolff, *The Polyglot Lovers,* trans. Saskia Vogel

73 Mario Levrero, *Empty Words,* trans. Annie McDermott

74 Michelle Tea, *Against Memoir*

75 Cristina Rivera Garza, *The Taiga Syndrome,* trans. Suzanne Jill Levine and Aviva Kana

76 Hanne Ørstavik, *Love,* trans. Martin Aitken

77 Tim Etchells, *Endland*

78 Rita Indiana, *Made in Saturn,* trans. Sydney Hutchinson

79 Luke Brown, *Theft*

80 Gerald Murnane, *Collected Short Fiction*

81 Gerald Murnane, *Invisible Yet Enduring Lilacs*

82 James Attlee, *Isolarion*

83 Deb Olin Unferth, *Barn 8*

84 Juan Pablo Villalobos, *I Don't Expect Anyone to Believe Me,* trans. Daniel Hahn

85 Andrzej Tichý, *Wretchedness,* trans. Nichola Smalley

86 Yuri Herrera, *A Silent Fury: The El Bordo Mine Fire,* trans. Lisa Dillman

87 Ann Quin, *Three*

88 Lina Wolff, *Many People Die Like You,* trans. Saskia Vogel

89 Claudia Hernández, *Slash and Burn,* trans. Julia Sanches

Born and raised in the Dominican Republic and now living in Puerto Rico, RITA INDIANA is a driving force in contemporary Caribbean literature and music. She is the author of three collections of stories and five novels. Three of her novels have been translated into English. *Papi* made *World Literature Today*'s 2016 list of 75 Notable Translations. *Tentacle*, published by And Other Stories, won the Grand Prize of the Association of Caribbean Writers, the first book written in Spanish to do so.

SYDNEY HUTCHINSON is an ethnomusicologist, folklorist, and pianist by training. She has published several books and numerous articles in both Spanish and English on Latin American and Caribbean music and dance. Currently living in Berlin, she spends her spare time yodeling and playing protest music on the accordion.